"Fans of Beautiful Disaster will love this one with Rocker boys, First love and page turning goodness. First Kiss is a must read…"

    ~ Bella, Paranormal Book Club

"While books have music as the theme, Frohoff takes it the next level by having a soundtrack with original music tied directly to the main character. Bringing the characters to life in a unique way. The music is the soul of the book. I not only hope this book and soundtrack will bring pleasure to many, I also hope that it raises awareness with its sensitive subject matter and maybe just maybe it might help save someone's life."

    ~ Amy Del Rosso, Publicist, Rhemalda Publishing Company

SKID OUT

A Heavy Influence Novella

By Ann Marie Frohoff

Book layout by www.ebooklaunch.com

AMF Publishing
Ann Marie Frohoff
heavyinfluencetrilogy@gmail.com

Second Digital Edition: December 2013

Frohoff, Ann Marie, 1971—
Skid Out : a novella / by Ann Marie Frohoff.—2nd edition

Summary: About an up and coming teenage rocker on the verge of
stardom, when the girl next door becomes something more; they're
forced to face the harsh realities on his road to fame and the
expectations of their friends and family. Sacrifices are made as
everything changes as they know it.

For everyone who has a dream,
without we would still be in the dark.

Thank you to my husband for allowing me to spread
my wings, believing in me that I'd find my way home
and to my daughter for allowing me to ask
way too many questions.

Thank you to Chris Bowman for lending your vision
and your voice to bring this story to life.

Thank you to Amy Del Rosso for being my number
one fan and believing in this story from its infancy
and for introducing me to so many wonderful
bookish people. You are the wind in my sails.
I could have not done this without you.

Thank you to all the book bloggers (and Twitter for
introducing us) who have embraced this story and for
your daily insight on all things bookish! Your devotion
and love of reading is so inspiring.

Thank you to Shaun Barger
for your endless support and expertise
and to Kim Tillman for your
constructive criticism and knowledge.

Special thanks to those who have given me the passion
to write so true (you know who you are);
I couldn't have done this without you.

...Art imitates life...
~ Oscar Wilde

1

JAKE

Have you ever wished you could take back a night? Wished you could at least forget it ever happened? That's how I felt, watching Rachel whiz around my bedroom. My head throbbed and I wanted to barf. Too much booze had me in a black hole and I'd hooked up with Rachel. After two years of keeping her at arm's length, she finally got to me. I wanted to fucking shoot myself.

"Do you see my shoes? Do you think they're in your car?" She chirped. Her mood was way too chipper for me and I hung my head, trying not to puke. "Aww baby. What's wrong?"

She sat down next to me, rubbing the top of my head. I stopped myself from pulling away, fighting the urge to be a dick. I wanted to blame the whole thing on her, but how lame would that be? What guy doesn't want a booty call? I shivered at the thought. What was I thinking? I didn't even like her like that.

"I wanna throw up, that's what's wrong." My head remained buried in my hands. I wanted to tell her it was a mistake. Maybe this would blow over and things would be like they were before. I could only hope. "What time is it? I have a meeting with a producer who came to the show last night."

She looked at her cell. "It's 9:30 AM."

Giving me a wet peck on the cheek, she got up and disappeared into the bathroom. I wiped her spit residue off my face with disgust and hoofed it out of my room to the kitchen. This could turn ugly, I thought. My mouth was as dry as the desert; I gulped down some Gatorade as I stood in front of the fridge. At least last night's show had gone well—we were on fire. I smiled, satisfied. It seemed like every one of my classmates had come to our show in Hollywood to kick off summer vacation. The place had been packed with familiar faces. We partied like the world was ending, even though it was really just beginning. We were all finally seniors.

Thankfully my mother wasn't home when Rachel finally left. I blamed our awkward goodbye on my hangover. Her normally painted face was clean from the dark eye makeup and red lipstick. This was the first time I'd seen her without her war paint on. She looked odd without it. As pretty as she was, there wasn't anything extraordinary about her. She wasn't a natural beauty; cute, yeah, but nothing special. She didn't do it for me, simple as that. What was that saying- don't shit where you sleep? Was that the right phrase for this? Ugh. Rachel was such a big part of my band life, and now this was gonna seriously screw things up. I just knew it.

Driving to West Hollywood was the last thing I wanted to do, bad as I felt. The summer heat was just beginning and it made my wooziness worse. I tried to focus on the task at hand. When I got to King's Road Café on Beverly Boulevard, the outside tables were packed. Every hipster in town must have been eating there. You couldn't help but feel self-conscious walking up. Everyone watched everyone else, wondering who was who, if they were anyone famous. I chuckled to myself at how new-age-twilight-zone the scene was, everyone with their hip clothes and their cool shades, trying to look like they weren't trying. It was a joke. The fact was, we were all trying. At least *I* could admit it.

I spotted Jeff and made a beeline for him. I could literally feel the eyes poking me as I passed by.

"Hey, man, thanks for driving up," he said, holding his hand out.

I gave him a firm shake and glanced around. "I don't think I'm cool enough to eat here."

He shrugged. "Just think of it as a bad 3D experience."

We both laughed.

"I have to admit though, I'm a little jealous of all the tattoo sportin' mo-fos." I said, opening the menu. "I want a sleeve on this arm."

He nodded. "You're gonna have to wait until you're eighteen, unless you can talk your mom into taking you to Arizona."

"No shit?"

"No shit," he said with raised eyebrows.

"I'm all over that. Next tour, it's on." My mood buoyed at the thought. I'd wanted the same tat for the last three years. I was pretty sure of my choice.

"When do you leave?"

"In a few weeks," I said, gulping down the glass of water that was placed in front of me.

My stomach rumbled with hunger, making me more nauseous. Thankfully my breakfast burrito didn't

3

take long. My mouth watered in anticipation of the first bite. We ate our food and talked about the band. Jeff was curious as to how we managed with all of us being in school. I explained that Bobby, Mike and I were toying with the idea of being home schooled our senior year if things kept going like they were. Dump, our drummer, was twenty—he didn't have to worry about school.

Jeff Arnault was a famous, Grammy-nominated producer. He was fairly young, in his late twenties, but he'd produced some of my favorite bands. I was beyond stoked that he felt us worthy of his attention. We made plans to record one song in his studio. I was on cloud nine when we got up to leave. We weaved our way through the closely arranged tables and chairs, trying not to bang into anyone. Once again everyone stared, watching us as we passed. I'd always gotten a lot of stares, mainly from chicks, but this was different; even the dudes were checking me out.

I stood next to my truck, staring back at the crowd outside, and wondered if I would ever be the guy everyone knew about. I didn't want to be famous for the sake of being famous. I wanted to be known for my music. I wanted to be the guy that these people pointed at and whispered about because of the songs I'd written. I could only pray, because there was no plan B.

I was finally feeling halfway human and continued to push Rachel from my mind. I hoped she wouldn't show up at band practice. I needed mass distance from that whole scenario. I tried to focus on thinking about the things I had to take care of before we left for tour as I dialed our manager. The call went straight to voice mail.

"Hey, Notting, it's Jake. Just wanted you to know I met with Jeff and we're good to go. We're going into the studio next week, stoked. Call me back, wanna talk about the new merch and if it's gonna be done in time."

Driving down my street, I spotted my next-door neighbor in the distance, Alyssa. She and her friends hung out on the corner across from my house nearly every day there wasn't school. I looked for her again as I got out of my truck. Checking her out, it struck me that I'd been admiring her more often than I cared to admit. I wondered how old she was. She looked at least fifteen, but I knew she couldn't be because she didn't go to my school yet. She reminded me of my ex-girlfriend, Renee, a younger version, but not as dark. Aly was definitely prettier than Renee. Her figure reminded me of a doe— slender and timid. I honed in on her laughter as I stood in my garage trying not to stare at her. It brought me back to when I used to be friends with her brother Kyle. I used to tickle her until she peed her pants. That was fucked, I thought, laughing.

I perched myself behind Dump's drum set and grabbed a set of sticks. I banged out a new beat that'd been ricocheting around in my head and watched Aly to see if it would grab her attention. She didn't even glance in my direction. Living next door to me all these years, she'd probably tuned out my playing by now.

Rachel pulled into my driveway, adding fuel to my uneasy mood. Of course she had to show up, I thought.

"Hey babe," she said loudly as she slammed her car door shut. I cringed. I didn't want anyone to hear her. I didn't want anyone to think she was my girlfriend. I looked out at the group across the street. No one seemed to pay attention.

"What's wrong with you?" she nipped. I quickly realized that she was wearing her bitch hat. Great, getting her to leave was not going to be fun.

Ignoring her, I banged hard on the drums, pretending that I didn't hear her. Finally, I looked at her. "What's up?"

I was being a dick and I didn't care.

Her face twisted. "Really?" She was ready to put me in my place, as always. She rolled her eyes at me. "You got an email with some dates and other things, so I just wanted to talk to you about it."

"You couldn't call?" I asked, agitated. "The guys are gonna be here any minute and I'm working on something. Can't this wait?"

Her mouth gaped open. "Is this how it's gonna be?" She folded her arms across her chest.

I sighed. She was right. I didn't have to be a douchebag. "Look, I'm sorry. I'm tired. I still feel like shit from last night." I paused, deciding to put our hook-up to rest. "Rachel, I don't remember last night. I don't wanna be that guy, ok. I don't remember being with you, and I feel like shit about it."

I put as good of a spin on it as I could. The fact was I did remember flashes, enough to send the eebies running through me. What the hell was wrong with me? Rachel turned heads when she walked into a room. She was hot, as far as my friends were concerned. I was a fool for not wanting her.

She sighed and her face grew softer. "I see. Well, I don't remember much either."

"Yeah, not how I like to roll." I looked around uncomfortably and tapped on the cymbal.

Awkwardness began to creep in. I didn't know what else to say. I wanted her to get it. I wanted her to read my mind and leave. Thankfully, Dump arrived and I stood up. I stared at Rachel without a word, and she finally conceded.

"Ok. Hope you feel better." She stood for a moment, waiting for me to come around from the drums, but I was planted firmly. It was different now. Normally I would hug her warmly, thanking her for being rad.

"I'll call you tonight after I get through this and catch a nap. Thanks Rach," I said, giving her a crooked smile. She turned, flipping her blond hair without a word. She wasn't happy.

Dump stood quiet, looking at me with a bent grin. "Dude, you fucked up, didn't you?"

"Beyond, man. Why didn't you stop me?" I threw the sticks across the garage. "I just have to hope she doesn't take this like we're going out now."

"Good luck with that," he laughed.

"I wanted to chew my arm off this morning."

Dump laughed harder. "What, it wasn't with a boner that you woke up to her snuggled next to you?"

"Dude, I coulda chewed my arm off and beat myself with it." I grabbed my hair, groaning.

Band practice went along like any other. As soon as I confirmed that I wasn't into Rachel, Mike, our other guitarist, gave me a good ribbing. He began to strum an impromptu tune about what he'd like to do to Rachel and he drilled me for info. I don't think I'd ever wanna do a girl that my friend just did, but we're talking about Mike here. He was on a different planet.

The next few days I avoided Rachel as much as I could, and tried to ease back into the way things were. Thankfully, she didn't put any pressure on me, but I knew that wouldn't last. Sooner or later she'd wanna hang—alone—and talk.

2

ALYSSA

Today was going to be different. I could feel it when I woke up. A strange excitement filled me—I couldn't put my finger on why. Maybe it's because I knew I'd be spending the whole summer with Matt. Or was it because I was finally gonna be in high school in a few short months? Nadine and I were the first to plant ourselves on the retaining wall across the street from my house. I wondered whose pool we'd infiltrate, or if we'd go down to the beach. I was antsy with anticipation of Matt's arrival. It was already hot. As ideal as Nicole's pool was, one of her older brothers could be such a jerk. He wasn't very accepting of us as a group. Our gang consisted of several guys. We were now a co-ed sampler of newly-minted high school freshman, and knowing him, it would just be one more reason to give us a hard time.

Greg Sanchez rolled up on his bike in all his plumpness. His jet-black hair made his fair skin look paler. His stomach spilled over his pants. Greg was interesting, his brothers had a huge influence on his behavior and he was always eager to share the going's on with them. It was gross and at the same time intriguing to listen to. Like the time he brought over his brother's video camera and showed us firsthand what'd gone down with a freshman in the boy's locker room. This one poor kid got all his clothes taken away behind his back as someone distracted him. He was left standing in his underwear and everyone was laughing at him. I guess they'd finally found his clothes in a trashcan across campus. That was the saddest thing to watch, and we all grew quiet with fear. In hushed tones, we wondered out loud how we'd get through our freshman year, especially the guys. Remembering their worried expressions made my stomach turn.

"What's up?" Greg said, nodding. I was happy to see him riding his bike; most of the time he had one of his brothers drive him over. He climbed off of his bike, letting it fall onto the sidewalk, and walked toward us. He stood there, breathing heavily, and lifted his t-shirt, wiping his sweaty face and exposing his pale white belly to us.

"Greg, you really need to get some sun on that thing. Your arms are super-tan and your stomach belongs somewhere else," Nadine said, crossing her arms in disgust.

"Nadine!" I choked, trying to not laugh. She was so abrupt and embarrassing sometimes. Well, *a lot* of the time.

"Well, it's true. Tan fat is better than white fat."

Greg lifted his shirt again, rubbing his stomach. "My food baby likes being white."

"In all seriousness, Greg, I also used to be chubby in grade school, but I got my shit together. Tan that thing or don't flash it at me." Nadine turned away, mock-gagging, and Greg laughed. I laughed too, nudging his arm. He was such a good sport—always taking everyone's shit.

"So what's going on?" Greg wondered aloud. "I need a pool, or let's go down to the beach."

"Not much. Did you go by Matt's house?" I asked casually, not making eye contact, worried he would read my mind if our eyes locked.

Thinking of Matt Squire with his bold green eyes made me warm inside. I totally crushed on Matt. He was fast becoming Abercrombie status. He was the only guy who made me nervous. I wondered when he'd show up.

"Nope, they went to Vegas," Greg answered, kicking the rocks around in the flowerbed next to the retaining wall. "What's going on today?"

My fire went out. I slumped, kicking my feet hard against the wall. I was bummed I wouldn't see Matt, and wondered how long he would be gone.

"I don't know," I said, sulking, "Beats me. We should go to Nicole's." I hopped off the wall, frustrated.

That's the moment my world began to change. Jake Masters, the boy next door, pulled into his driveway. I'd known Jake practically my entire life. He's someone who'd spent the night at my house, sleeping next to me, piled on the floor in front of the TV. Nadine perked up instantly, fluffing her hair while glancing down at her chest. I then glanced down at mine, and back at hers. She pulled down on her tank top to show off her boobs a bit more. I looked back down at my chest. *What the?* I thought. *What's she doing?* I glanced in Jake's direction, I didn't think he noticed us.

When Jake was home, he was always out in his garage. He was either rehearsing with his band or tooling around with his truck. He never said anything to us besides a *"Hey"* or a head nod from time to time. Jake would small talk my dad when he watered the lawn. Jake and I would chat every now and then, but for the most part, we kept to ourselves. Jake was older than me. He was now a senior and he same age as my brother, Kyle. Jake and my brother used to be close, but Kyle went the nerd route and Jake went the wannabe rock star route.

I watched Nadine mess with her clothes and hair. "What are you doing?" I giggled under my breath.

"What?" she whispered loudly, tossing her hair to one side and puffed her chest out more.

I fluffed my own hair, mocking her. "This," I said. I puffed up my chest, looking over at Jake.

Then as we both stared at him, he took off his shirt, throwing it over onto the nearby lawn. Nadine and I stared in awe. Watching him hose down his truck half-naked made the world stop. I glanced back at Nadine, who had her mouth wide open, nearly drooling.

I looked at Greg, remembering that he was there. I was a little embarrassed. He glanced between Jake and us.

"Uh, you guys are weird," he said, uncomfortably, "I'm outta here. I'll meet you at Nicole's."

He rode away and I began to laugh, but Nadine didn't notice, her eyes were intently placed on Jake.

"Dude, what are you doing?" I murmured. "Do you like him or something? Do you want me to introduce you?" As long as I've known Nadine, she never acted this way towards Jake. I'd never realized she even knew he existed.

Nadine sat back on the wall and started to laugh loudly. I looked at her like she'd gone crazy and she leaned over to me, whispering, "Just go along with me."

I started laughing loudly, too. Sure enough, Jake looked over and smiled at us. I felt like an idiot.

"God, he's so freakin' hot," she said under her breath, nearly hyperventilating.

I laughed loudly, for real this time.

Jake smirked as he continued washing his big black truck, glancing from time to time at us. "You girls wanna share what's so funny?" he shouted. Nadine turned, eye-balling me, and I turned to face Jake.

"You want some help?" I shouted back. He stopped washing and offered the most brilliant smile I'd ever seen.

Jake shrugged his shoulders. "Sure, if you guys wanna help…that'd be cool."

Nadine nudged me with a wicked grin, striding ahead of me. I quickly followed behind her and we crossed the street without a word.

I awkwardly cleared my throat, introducing them to each other. "Jake, this is Nadine," I said, giving a weak smile. "She lives around the corner." I raised my arm and pointed, waving it around like a spaz.

He cracked a brilliant smile again. "Yeah, I've seen you before," he said. "You go to my school. What's up?"

Jake nodded his head as he examined us a bit more closely. His eyes parked themselves on mine and my stomach went nuts. I began to fidget with my shirt, look-ing away briefly. Jake looked around awkwardly too, and laughed a little.

"Wha'cha guys up to this sweltering morning?" He turned and walked into his garage, grabbing two rags and raised them up.

"Not much." I croaked out.

He threw each of us a rag and resumed scrubbing his truck. Nadine mouthed *"Oh my freakin' God!"* and turned, dipping her rag into the bucket. I stood there dumbfounded. This was new to me, the whole manipulating the situation thing. I'd only seen it on TV. Now we were the characters.

"So, Jake, how's the band doing?" I tried to make small talk as I diligently washed the windows on the other side of the truck; but at the same time I really did wonder. I glanced into the garage. "Looks like your garage has turned into a professional studio, what's that stuff on the walls?"

He looked up, wiping his damp brow with his forearm. "That's sound proofing foam. It's as sound proof as I can it get for now *and* the band is doing great," he explained, walking toward me. "We just had a show at the Roxy in Hollywood. You should come to the next one."

My heart began to race and my throat thickened. All I could do was gulp, trying to find moisture. He finally continued, taking the pressure off.

"We're a lot better than you probably remember," he said, coming closer to me. He tossed his rag back and forth between his hands while his eyes scanned my face. "Look at you, you've grown up."

Like a loud gong, Nadine's voice rang out. "Yeah, we'd love to come and see you play." She rounded the backside of the truck, standing a little too close to Jake.

He backed away, looking her up and down. "Uh, yeah, anytime, just let me know."

"Hey, would you like me to rinse the soap?" Nadine asked, grabbing the hose off the ground.

"Yeah, before it dries, that'd be cool," he said, flashing a wink at her.

What the hell? Was he flirting with her? I glanced at Nadine as she began to squirt the bubbles off of Jake's truck and I wondered if she saw what I saw.

"God, it's so hot," she said, holding the bright yellow nozzle over her head, squirting water straight up into the air. I squealed as it rained down on us and dashed over to the manicured lawn grabbing Jake's shirt from the ground, holding it over my face.

"Ahhh, shit," Jake shouted, laughing loudly. "Nadine, be careful of the garage!" he warned and jogged to the sidewalk, guiding Nadine's direction of waterworks.

Abercrombie, most definitely, I thought, staring at Jake's glistening wet torso. God, I'd never noticed how studly he was. His muscular build left me speechless. Covering my mouth, I giggled, and he took notice.

"What? You think you're gonna stay dry?" He shouted, running toward me. He grabbed my waist, twirling me around—then held me in a tight bear hug up off the ground.

"Nadine! Let her have it!"

The water rained down on us, and then fell directly upon me, stinging my skin. Jake held me tightly to his chest. I could barely move; squealing and laughing so hard I almost peed. I buried my face into his shirt, which I still held in my hands. Jake finally released me and I ran across the street, avoiding any more water games.

"You bitch!" I shouted through fits of laughter and leaned against the wall trying to catch my breath. I was soaking wet.

Jake ran after Nadine, grabbing the hose from her. He held her wrists together with one hand while he used his free one to soak her down. She didn't fight to get away like I did. She clearly liked the attention. Jake stopped and stared over at me. I was surprised to see how much taller he was than Nadine. Nadine had always been taller than me; I was already 5'8. I considered both of us pretty tall. Jake must be over six feet tall...— his voice shook me from my thoughts.

"Ok," Jake shouted over at me, "I promise we won't water fight anymore. Come back and help dry."

Sopping wet, Nadine futilely tried to fluff her hair. I walked back over, giving her a defiant smile, and she winked at me, satisfied. I was both relieved and feeling a little of something else I couldn't pinpoint.

"Be right back." Jake announced, going into his garage and vanished into his house.

"Oh my *God*, he is so to die for!" Nadine swooned against the truck. "When he was holding me back from squirting you, I wanted him to pin me against this truck and kiss me," she confessed. "You have to find out the deets on what's up with him."

My chin must have hit the ground. "What do you mean?" I said, pretending I didn't get where she was headed and dried my arms and then face with his shirt. I noticed how nice it smelled and took in a deeper whiff; my eyes rolled back into their sockets. "Dude, you gotta smell this!"

Nadine took a quick sniff and grabbed the shirt out of my hands, stuffing her face in it. Jake unexpectedly walked out his front door and we both spun around to face him. Nadine tossed his shirt onto the hood of the truck.

"Here ya go. I just pulled them out of the dryer." He handed each of us a warm towel. "After you're done drying yourselves, you can use them to dry the truck. Oh, and make sure you don't touch the tires. My mom'll kill me if I get black stains on them."

As he turned back to shut the front door, I quickly reached up and grabbed his shirt, tucking it into the back of my shorts.

We heard a shout from down the street. *"Nadine!"* and could see her mother wearing a bright red caftan and black leggings as she stood on the sidewalk, looking for her. *"Nadine!"* she shouted again.

"Shit! Shit! I totally forgot," Nadine said in a panic. "I forgot I have a dentist appointment." Glancing down at her watch she went on, "Now I'll have to change and we're gonna be late. She's going to kill me! I'll see you at Nicole's later." She threw the towel at us and turned, running home.

"OK," I shouted after her. I stood there in silence, feeling weird and suddenly self-conscious. I looked over to Jake, shrugging my shoulders. He smiled back and continued to dry his truck.

As watched Jake from the other side of the truck, his bare chest rubbed against the window as he dried the roof. The sight made me weak. I felt like a total perv, but I couldn't take my eyes off him. Then suddenly he opened the door and I quickly looked away, praying to God he hadn't seen me ogling his all-too-perfect frame. He stepped up into the cab and continued drying the roof. My heart raced. All I could see were his impossibly firm waist muscles shifting under his smooth, lightly tanned skin; I nearly jumped out of my own skin when his voice sounded.

"So, little Miss Alyssa Montgomery, what have you been up to all this time?" he asked. "You're nearly all grown up."

Laughing nervously, I fumbled for words. "Uh, well, just super stoked to finally be starting high school," I stuttered, walking over to his side of the truck. I inspected his work, as if I really cared. "I've been taking piano lessons, playing volleyball and just hanging out, really, not much else. What else is up with you?"

Jake was quiet for a few moments as his eyes searched my face. I felt the heat rising in my cheeks. I wanted to die.

Finally he spoke. "Besides rehearsing like a madman with the band and just barely getting through school, you're lookin' at it," he said. "Not sure if you knew, but we kinda been doin' little mini-tours. So I've been missing a lot of school, but I managed to eek out getting into the 12th grade." A proud grin stretched across his too handsome face.

"How does your mom feel about you eeking by?" I asked curiously, "my parents would kick my ass if I got anything below a B."

"By *eeking* I mean I'm not an A student, more like a solid B, some C's. I think with everything that goes on with the band, she's just happy I'm making it through." He shrugged. "You know, we have a pretty beefy tour lined up this summer, so I'm stoked."

His eyes sparkled when he spoke. I never noticed how blue they were, especially in contrast with his dyed-black hair. Jake used to have light brown, nearly blond hair. Then one day it was black, and he's never gone back.

"Wow, Jake, I had no idea. I feel bad for not paying attention," I said, shamefaced. "Does your band have a website?"

"Yeah, wanna come in and check it out?"

My insides tumbled around as I stared back at him. Nadine was right. He really was to die for. "Um, sure."

I knew his mom wasn't home. I assumed she was working and his dad had passed away when he was younger. I barely remembered his dad. Taking in a deep breath, I calmed myself. What the hell did I think would happen anyway? Stupid Nadine, this was all her fault. Ok, *breathe deeply*, I told myself. Desperately trying to stay calm. Like an out-of-body experience, I saw myself running across our lawns into my house.

"Are you ok?" he asked with concern in his eyes.

My frantic thoughts stopped in their tracks. "Yeah. I was just thinking if there was anything I needed to do."

"Alright, cool." He turned, leading the way into the house.

I continued to fight the voices in my head, trying not to look like a schizophrenic. Besides, whom was I kidding? I was no match for Nadine and her big boobs. Boys loved boobs. Not to mention all the hot chicks who were always hanging around Jake. *The Envies,* as we underclassmen called them.

I guess I'd been paying attention to a portion of Jake's life instead of Jake himself. But now that Nadine had shed light on him, my eyes were wide open.

3

ALYSSA

I hadn't been inside of Jake's house in over two years. We walked through the foyer and into the living room. I was shocked by the change. I didn't recognize one thing from years ago. The inside was totally remodeled. Gone was the 60's-ish shag carpet, replaced with dark hardwood floors and the drab gray sofas had been replaced with dark tanned leather ones, they looked expensive and totally plush. A huge TV, the size of a bay window, covered the far wall. And an electronic stereo system stared back at me menacingly.

Note to self: Never Touch That.

The other wall, while once solid, now had windows allowing a view of the pool and backyard. The backyard appeared to be the same. It had always been landscaped like an oasis, with huge banana trees, ivy, and those sweet-smelling gardenia flowers. I loved his backyard—it reminded me of being poolside in Hawaii.

"The computer's in my room," he said, walking ahead of me. "Oh, take the slaps off. Kate doesn't want us grimmin' up or scuffin' her shit. Like rubber will scuff, but whatever." He shrugged, and a flash of irritation ran across his face.

I stopped just short of the earth-tone runner leading toward the hallway. "Oh, ok," I said, kicking off my flip-flops. "Hey, just curious, why do you call your mom by her name?"

Jake looked at me with hooded eyes and a bent smile. "Because when we're out doin' band shit, the last thing I wanna shout out is—*Hey Mom*—so, naturally." He shrugged. "And at this point, I prefer it."

Walking over the yummy rugs in my bare feet, I could feel why Kate didn't want them messed up, I sank in an inch they were so deluxe. We continued down the hallway until we reached a door at the end of the hall. Jake had changed rooms. He used to be in the closest room to his mom's; now he was the farthest. The first thing I'd noticed was a French door opened at the other end of the room and it led out to the backyard. A hot tub was just to the right of it. *What a guy*, I thought. Of course he'd want this room. I would.

"Wow, this is cool. When did you switch rooms?" I said, marveling at how neat everything was. Matt's room was a messy piece of shit compared to this. "I would die to have a hot tub right next to my room." I fawned and turned looking around. "Dude, you have your own bathroom, too!" I walked from one side to the other, scanning every inch of every surface, twirling and landed on his bed, crossing my legs up underneath me. I batted my eyes. "I'll trade you."

"Ha, I'm sure you would," he said, pensively. His eyes locked on mine and my hands went numb. He flashed his perfect smile at me and shook his head. "Is your dad still a hard-ass?"

"Yep, the older I get, the more of a hard-ass he is. My poor guy friends don't even come to the door

anymore. They just hang on the corner until I come out."
I laughed at the thought. But it wasn't funny. He was
way too strict, and because of it, my brother, sister and I
always lied to him. "But he loves me, so what can I do?"

"You can't do anything, and I see why he's such a
hard-ass." My hands tingled hearing his words.

Was that a compliment? Why would he say it like
that? I felt the heat start to rise in my face.

"What?" A smile peaked at the corners of his mouth.

"Nothing." I laughed nervously, shaking my head.
My spastic insides were getting the best of me, and I got
up to look out into the backyard. Oh my God, I knew
he totally caught me staring at him like an idiot. I scram-
bled to find anything to move me from my
embarrassment and turned to face him. "When ya gonna
pull up that music?"

"Hello, can't you see I'm booting up my computer?"
He replied, playfully and gestured to me. "See, clearly
this is why your dad is a hard ass."

Finally, in a more neutral mood I walked over to Jake
and bent down, leaning over his shoulder as he pulled up
his band website. I was impressed. It was done up professional, just like all the other hot bands out there. There
was his picture, as big as life, staring back at me like someone I didn't know. He clicked on the music player and
turned up the volume. Unfamiliar sounds streamed out of
the speakers; a guitar riff and keyboard melody drifted out
over the room. Drumbeats followed, and then a voice, a
voice I didn't recognize. I really liked it. It had an alterna-
tive rock-punky vibe. I closed my eyes.

"So, who's singing?"

"It's me! Duh!"

My eyes shot open. "No!" I shouted, "Oh my God! You sound so good, like so old! I mean not like an old man or anything. Wow, you totally kill it!" I was completely floored. Nadine was going to shit a brick when she heard him.

Jake lowered the music and spun around in his chair to face me and I stepped away from him. I couldn't take my eyes off him. I kept taking in slow deep breaths to steady my racing pulse and without a word he got up and walked out of the room. I took this opportunity to look around more closely. The walls were plastered with posters of rock bands, surf shots, and bikini girls. The bikini girls were of all types. I couldn't tell what kind of girl he was into and I wondered if he had a girlfriend. I snooped around to see if he had pictures with any girls lying around—anything to identify a special someone. I only found party pics and band snapshots. Yes, there were girls, and two of them were in most of the shots. Hmm, I wondered.

I sat down on the bed just as Jake came through the door. My insides were tense, and it made me fidgety. He was carrying a bag and some water.

"You thirsty?"

I nodded my head *yes*. Why was I speechless? Come on, Aly, its only Jake, I reminded myself. Get over it.

He tossed me a small bottle of water and sat down next to me. I nearly drank the whole bottle of water in one gulp.

"Shit, you were thirsty! You want more?" he offered and pulled what appeared to be t-shirts out of the bag.

I licked my lips. "No thanks, this is good. I didn't realize how parched I was."

Jake stopped and stared at me with a crooked grin. We were only inches apart, and his blue eyes took my breath away. I wiped my mouth with the back of my hand. I swore I had to have been drooling.

"Parched, huh? Who says that?" he teased. "That's a word my grandma uses." I giggled. I was okay with him teasing me. It pulled any weirdness out of the room.

"I read a lot, for your information. English literature is my fave." I tried to think of something else to add, but nothing came to mind and I leaned into him with my shoulder, "so there."

The scent, his scent, from his shirt caught my attention. God that smell was going to be the death of me. None of the guys we hung out with smelled as good.

"I wanted to give you some merch," he said, holding up a black t-shirt with the words *Rita's Revolt* printed in bold white letters. "And some CDs. You can pass these singles out to your friends, and you can have these," he said, holding up hard CD cases.

I grabbed the t-shirt and held it up, staring at it more closely.

"Jake, I'm super impressed. I really had no idea. I know I keep sayin' that, but geez." I remarked, smiling at the t-shirt and a shock of electricity shot through me when he touched my knee and thanked me.

"Tell me more about what you've been up to." He asked and his hand remained on my knee. "You say you read English literature—like what?"

This time he wasn't being a smartass. I leaned back against the pile of pillows, putting my arms behind my head and he pulled his hand away. Relief washed over me.

"Well, I really like Jane Austen. I'm a little embarrassed to admit it, but I really like those old-time, long ago romance novels." I paused. "The kind where the guy is chivalrous. Guys seem to be such jerks these days. You know, our friend Greg, Greg Sanchez, the bigger one? The stories he shares with us about his brothers—it's like shock factor or something."

"Oh, I know exactly who you're talking about and yeah, I agree. Those guys are idiots, and they think their shit doesn't stink. A bunch of jock dorks." He shook his head. "Not sure what's up with Greg being so fat, knowing how his sporto brothers are built. I fucking hate sportos." He frowned. "So, what kind of stories has Greg told you?"

I pondered for a moment if I should tell him. What the heck, I thought; it would be nice to have someone other than a bunch of 14-year-olds to give perspective. I mean, Greg could be lying for all I knew.

"Well," I started laughing nervously. "I don't know." I squirmed, and his smile grew bigger.

"Look at you, you're blushing!" He grabbed my shoulder and his face fell flat. He leaned in closer, super serious. "What's tubby telling you anyway? I wanna know if he's feeding you a bunch of bullshit." Jake's intensity surprised me. He got up sitting back at his desk and leaned way back in his chair, waiting for my answer.

"Jake, don't embarrass me. I feel silly even talking about it with you." I looked down at my feet. "I mean, he just tells us stories about how they bet on how many blow jobs they can get—"

Jake interrupted me right away.

"Ok, so this is *really* what you talk about with the guys you hang out with? Blow jobs?" Jake was aghast.

"Do you even know what that is? I'm no expert on when chicks start learning this shit. I never talked about this stuff with girls."

"Yes. I know what it is."

"OK, well let's hear it." He didn't smile or flinch.

I stared at Jake, completely horrified. I couldn't believe the direction our conversation had gone. My face must have said it all and we sat there in silence for what seemed like forever, staring at each other. Finally, he spun around to face his computer.

"Alyssa, don't always believe what you hear. Guys talk shit, they make stuff up and they lie," he said, while he typed. "Trust me. I used to make shit up all the time. I know it was only a few years ago."

"You mean you lie? About what?"

"No, not anymore, but when I was your age I did it to make me seem cooler. It's stupid, but whatevs." He spun back around to face me. "But this is just between you and me, of course. Your brother and I use to make shit up all the time."

"You're kidding!" I laughed out loud. "My nerd brother? Come on, you have to tell me, what did you guys used to say?"

"Dude, your brother isn't *that* big of a nerd, and I'm not telling you anything," he said, waving the palms of his hands at me. "I plead the fifth."

I was lost in his eyes again, along with his dashing smile. Contemplating his words: *I plead the fifth*, I tried to remember where I'd heard that and what it meant. "Plead the fifth?"

"What?"

"What does that mean?"

"It means that you aren't going to say anything because it might incriminate you, or be used against you at a later date. It's a law thing." He nodded his head and his eyes narrowed.

Just as he was about to go on, we heard Jake's name being shouted from the other room. Jake hung his head. "Looks like the guys are here to rehearse," he said, jumping up, "Don't forget the bag."

He waited for me to grab the bag and followed me out the door. As we rounded out of the hallway a group of *almost* equally good-looking guys stood staring back at us. They had bags of fast food in their hands.

"'Sup, bro," piped one with bleached blonde hair and intense blue eyes. He stuffed French fries in his mouth as he eyeballed me with a stupid smirk. I could only imagine what I looked like with my hair all rumbled and matted to my head.

"Alyssa, this is Mike," Jake said, pointing at smirk boy, "and that's Bobby, and Victor, but we call Vic 'Dumpster' or 'Dump'." Jake laughed. "But don't ask why we call him that."

"Sup, Alyssa?" Mike nodded as he chewed open-mouthed, looking me up and down.

I could tell right away Mike was a force.

"Hi," I squeaked out. I stood unmoving, like a statue and knew if I didn't get out of there pronto, they'd all notice I was blushing.

What the fuck, why was this happening?

"Uh…ok…Jake," I said nervously, "um, nice meeting you guys." I waved, walking toward the door, searching my pockets for my phone. "Oh, I left my phone in your room." Of course I did, I thought, mortified that I had to be there even a second longer.

I quickly walked past everyone, practically running down the hallway into his room. The smell of him hit me like a baseball bat. What was that scent? I grabbed my phone from the bed and looked around for anything to give me a clue. I saw a bottle of whatever it was, but I couldn't read it. The writing was all in French. I sniffed the bottle. That was it, God it smelled good. I took one last big breath in and walked out as calm as possible. I was probably as red as a tomato.

Walking down the hall I could hear them talking and it was about me. I stopped to eavesdrop.

"*So dude, ya doin' them younger these days I see.*"

"*Shut the fuck up, Mike, she's my next-door neighbor,*" Jake spat back.

"*That makes it convenient,*" Mike laughed. "*Yeah, clearly virgin territory.*"

"*I'm not doin' her, you fuck, get your mind outta the gutter.*"

I was even more mortified now and came out swiftly, not looking at anyone. "Alright, later," I waved. As soon as the door shut behind me, I sprinted across our front lawns, into my house. My sister was sitting on the sofa, watching TV. She didn't look in my direction. I ran up the stairs, colliding with my brother as he came out of the bathroom.

"Wow, man, slow down," Kyle said holding me by the shoulders. "Where's the fire?"

"Sorry, Kyle, I'm supposed to be at Nicole's right now. I got side-tracked." I explained, trying to squirm away.

"Hmm, what's in the bag?" he asked, letting me out of his tight grip. He grabbed the bag out of my hand and pulled out a t-shirt. "Ah, Jake's band…these are cool. Is there one for me?"

Kyle dropped the bag on the hallway floor and started pulling everything out.

"I'm sure there's one in there." I growled, stalking off to my room. I slammed the door. He irritated me.

I rummaged through my drawers until I found my bathing suit and gathered my stuff together. Taking off my shorts, Jake's shirt fell to the ground. I picked it up and stuffed my face into it. Gah, *that* smell. I collapsed onto my bed and firmly held it to my face as if my life depended on it. All of a sudden Kyle barged in, throwing the bag right onto my stomach, startling me.

"What are you doing?" he snickered.

"Nothing, just wiping my nose." I said, as my heart nearly sprung out of my throat.

Oh my God! What did it look like I was doing?

"Ugh, stay away from me!" he said, scowling and swiftly shutting the door.

After a moment of thinking *what the heck*, I put on my bathing suit and stuffed my things in a bag, along with Jake's shirt. I wanted Nicole to smell how yummy he was. Grabbing the bag of Jake's promo stuff, I bound down the stairs. I abruptly stopped before the door, staring at myself in the foyer mirror one last time. I didn't have a shirt on, only a bikini top. Should I put a shirt on? Ugh, why should I care? We live at the beach. Normally I wouldn't put one on.

As I opened the gate to leave my courtyard, my heart stopped. I felt lightheaded as soon as I saw Jake standing at the sidewalk, next to his truck. I didn't think I'd see him again so soon. Mike spotted me first and whistled. That made Jake turn to face me and he watched me walk toward him.

Why now? Why didn't I ever notice Jake like this before? I thought of Nadine. I could never admit that I was now crushing on Jake Masters. Nadine would beat my ass. I would be labeled as one of those girls who backstabbed her friends. She had first dibs. She saw him first. That was the rule. This was easy, though, because my dad would never approve of a senior, and me, even if it were Jake. I laughed at how quickly the fantasy rushed through my head. As if. I walked closer to Jake and his smile burned into me like a red-hot poker.

"Well, well, well, you comin' over to go swimmin'?" he asked playfully, holding his hands out at me. "Just another reason your father has become more of a hard-ass."

He made my knees go weak and my throat go dry. The cat calling continued as I passed by. All I wanted to do was run screaming down the street. I could still feel Jake's eyes on me the further away I walked. It was like an invisible string pulled at me to turn my head. I didn't dare to. *Don't do it*, I told myself—but I couldn't help it. When I looked over my shoulder, our eyes met and he gave me one last wave.

"Hey, I really want to know what you think of that music! Come by later," he shouted, giving me his heart-stopping smile.

What the hell was I going to tell Nadine?

As soon as I turned the corner and was out of Jake's sight, I sped up my pace. My heart raced and my thoughts swirled uncontrollably. The thought of him asking me to come back over sent my mind reeling. Why would he ask me that if he didn't want me around, right? Whatever it was, I could never admit my feelings to Nadine or any of the others. First, because of Matt, and second, all the others had big mouths. Nadine would find out in no time.

I hadn't notice that my pace slowed to a near stand-still as I daydreamed about Jake in front of Nicole's house. There was no turning back.

4

ALYSSA

I finally cleared my head enough to walk into Nicole's house. Nicole Hamilton and I had been best friends since the 4th grade. Her delicate, doll-like features and saucer-wide blue eyes were a contrast to my tall-thin build, brown hair and eyes.

I opened the front door and a blast of cool air slapped me in the face. I loved the air-conditioning. We didn't turn ours on throughout the day - "*It's too expensive*", my mother would say. Nicole's family had lots of money. I had to admit, I was jealous. She got whatever she wanted.

Nadine wasn't there yet. Nicole's brothers, Stephen and Chris, were hanging out in the family room, watching TV. I crawled up onto the stairs, sitting midway up, which gave me a clear view of them and of the backyard, too. It was around 11:30 in the morning, and it was already 90 degrees. This was not normal Southern California beach weather. I looked through the sliding glass door, and Greg was chasing Grant, squirting him with the hose. I could see Nicole lying out, getting a tan.

"Hey Alyssa," Stephen said. Chris didn't look at me. Chris was the best-looking brother, and he knew it, too.

Stephen had an offbeat good look and wore his hair longer, dressing like those eclectic hot Euro boys. Chris was sporty, the jock, and it was all about him.

"Hi." I smiled, holding the railing above my head with both hands. I leaned my head through the bars. "It's so effing hot outside, and I'm not ready to go melt yet. Do you mind if I sit here for a minute?"

"Nope, feel free to sit as long as you'd like." Stephen got up and walked into the kitchen. My mother would sell her soul for their kitchen, with its grey granite counters and one of those industrial stoves. The fridge was one that looked like cabinets, and it was doublewide. "You want something to drink?" Stephen offered. "Cut the dust?"

"Yes, please."

"What's your vice?"

"Vice?" I tilted my head.

"Vice means—hmm, how do I explain this?" He placed both hands on the counter looking down. "It means what's your weakness, or what is it that you like the most. I think." He stared up at me, smiling.

"Ok, good enough," I laughed. "I'll take a Coke if you've got it."

"Yep." He walked over to the fridge.

I was now looking at guys in a new light. I noticed how muscular Stephen's arms were, and compared him to Jake. His t-shirt fit nicely over his biceps and chest— something I would have never noticed before. I admired his face as he turned around. I smiled at him when he reached up to hand me the soda. Our eyes locked for a second, and my stomach flipped.

What the heck?

"Thanks, Stephen." I was lost for any other words.

"Uh, yeah, of course," his lips curled slightly upward. He stared at me for a moment longer before he turned around.

I became self-conscious with that totally weird moment. What the hell was going on? Was I emitting some new vibe? I sat there drinking my soda, looking over the can, now focusing on Chris. Nadine crushed hard on Chris, too. I wondered how the Jake thing would play out because of that. Come to think about it, Nadine crushed on all the hot guys. She was completely boy crazy.

I never gave it too much thought until today, until the electricity had surged through me during our water fight. Why was I noticing guys in a different light now than I had before? I couldn't wait for Nadine to show up. I wanted to know when she first felt that intense attraction for a guy, if she ever felt what I was feeling. I ran through our fake conversation in my head. I'd play it off like I was envious.

I hopped down the stairs and through their family room. Chris finally noticed me and nodded a hello. I slid open the door leading to the backyard. Nicole laid face down across a lounge with her bathing suit pulled up her butt and her top untied.

"So, since when do you pull your bathing suit up your ass?" I asked playfully as I approached.

She lifted her head, squinting. "Since Stacey was over here laying out, and I saw what she did. She didn't have a lame big butt tan line or any lines on her back." Nicole buried her face back down in her towel.

"Shit it's hot out here." I pulled my towel out of my bag, and Jake's shirt came out with it. "Oh my God, dude, you have to smell this." I was giddy. I tossed the shirt near her head. She looked up. "Guess whose shirt that is?"

She took a little sniff. "Uh, yum!" she smiled and took another whiff. "This *is* yummy. Ok, I'm going to gross out if it's your brother's. Whose is it?"

"You know my next door neighbor?"

"Uh, yeah, how could I not notice Rocker Abercrombie?" she remarked.

Was I stuck in some sort of a bubble? I watched Nicole rub her face all over Jake's shirt again.

"Well, you won't be surprised, but Nadine is totally crushing on him." I reached over and grabbed the shirt out of her hands, stuffing it back into my bag. She gave me her pouty face. "Sorry, I'll have to give it back."

"Ok, spit it out, all the juicy details. How'd you get his shirt?" Her eyes flashed wide with intrigue.

I sat and told the story, giving her a play by play of every moment, with the exception of my feelings for Jake. I painted a vivid picture of how hot he looked dripping wet. I hedged a bit, not knowing if I should continue.

"Ok and…spit it out already," she said impatiently.

"Ok, ok." I giggled louder, covering my mouth. "Basically, I used his shirt to dry off my face and I kept it."

"And, tell me, how did Nadine act? You know, she kills me sometimes how she throws herself at guys." She rolled her eyes, shaking her head. *Boom*, there it was, another snide remark tossed at Nadine. Nicole had been tossing out subtle digs about Nadine more often these days, but I refused to bite. I didn't want to choose sides.

"No, she didn't throw herself on Jake. She didn't have a chance. Her mom came looking for her. She said she would be here after her doctor's appointment."

I finally laid down on a lounge. I was sweating from the heat. The sun burned at my skin, feeling kind of good, like a massage. Even knowing that I would pay for the sun damage later in life, I didn't care. I didn't use sunscreen. I loved having that sun-kissed look.

All of sudden, water came our way from Greg and Grant.

"Stop it, you a-hole!" Nicole roared. She didn't like to get her hair or face wet. In fact, when she swam, she only went in the water up to her chin.

"Calm down, sorry," Grant said, trying not to laugh. "What's up with you guys today, all secretive n'shit?"

"Let's go, they're talking about Jake Masters," Greg said, spilling the beans.

"What? Jake? That fucking wannabe. He sucks, and so does his band," Grant spewed as he climbed out of the pool. My blood boiled at the insult.

"Shut the eff up," I snapped. "You're just jealous because you can't play your stupid guitar as good as he can."

I was shocked at the harsh words that rolled out of my mouth and instantly regretted it. Nicole's mouth gaped open. Greg, with his usual timid self, backed away from our confrontation. I felt bad. Grant had tried out for Jake's band six months prior. I never gave it much thought until now. Grant didn't get picked, and I knew how badly he wanted it.

"You're a bitch, Alyssa." He picked up his towel and wiped his face. "I was only joking."

I realized at that moment he had to be kidding, because he would have never tried out to be in the band if he thought it sucked.

"Dude, I'm sorry." My stomach sank.

Grant hung his towel around his neck as he slipped on his flip-flops.

"Ok, you guys, just calm down. Grant, please don't leave," Nicole begged. She struggled to retie her bathing suit top, instead opting to gather the towel to her chest as she reached out toward Grant.

"I'll be back," he said to Nicole and threw me an angry glance. "I'm gonna go find Greg."

Grant went after Greg down the side of the house. We heard him shouting Greg's name.

"What the hell, dude. What was that?" Nicole glared at me. "You didn't have to say that shit."

"I'm sorry, I didn't mean it…"

"Uh, yes you did. I've never heard one mean word ever cross your lips, Alyssa. So don't tell me you didn't mean it. You shoulda seen your face. You know how bad he wanted to be in Jake's band. I can't believe you."

She got up and stormed into the house, leaving me sitting there in the blistering heat. My head spun. I felt panic rushing through me. Shit, now what? I'd managed to piss everyone off, all because of Jake Masters, in less than an hour. My thoughts went back to Jake. I wanted to be sitting in his room, lying on his bed, smelling his scent. If his friends hadn't shown up, I would have probably been doing just that.

I gathered my things and walked into the house. Chris and Stephen were no longer around. Nicole stood at the fridge leaning against it with a soda in hand, glaring at me.

"I'm really sorry," I said in a rush. "I don't know what came over me." I played with the handles of my bag. "I didn't get to finish my story. You wanna know?"

"Uh, yeah," she said theatrically. As if she'd forgotten my verbal bashing of Grant.

The lameness was instantly gone. I took a deep breath, smiling. "Ok. I was with Jake in his room, listening to his music…and, you know how close we used to be…" I paused.

Nicole stared off in the distance. She was no longer listening to me. She took a drink of her soda and set it on the counter, pulling her long hair out of her face. I admired how pretty she was, with her all-American, blond hair and blue eyes. No wonder Grant kissed her ass. He probably felt like he hit the lottery.

I sighed, totally not into saying anything about Jake any more until Nadine got there. "Hey, just so you know, I'll call Grant later to apologize and I'll just talk to you about Jake later. I'm gonna go home for a bit. Call me when Nadine gets here. I wanna hear what she has to say about Jake. Plus, she'll wanna know what we did after she left." I flashed a wicked grin, trying to lighten the mood.

She snapped out of her mood and whined. "Oh come on! There's gotta be more. I was listening, I swear, you have to share!"

I laughed. "It's nothing, trust me. Other than Nadine's slice on it—and I can't wait to hear it."

5

ALYSSA

I glanced at the clock as I walked out of Nicole's house. Not very much time had gone by. I wondered if Jake was home and if he was still rehearsing. As I got closer to my house, I could hear the band playing. I arrived and stood in front of his house. I could hear his voice singing out, and it made me melt. He sounded older when he sang. I leaned against his truck. They played through two songs while I stood there in my dream state.

All of a sudden, the garage started to open, and I darted as quickly as I could toward my house.

"Hey, back already?" Jake called out and my knees buckled, making me stop. He opened the door to his truck, taking out a duffle bag and what appeared to be a camera tripod.

"Ha, yeah, I kinda got in an argument with one of the guys." I informed, throwing out my hands.

"Bummer," he said. He spoke again with his head down, muttering something as he struggled with the bag and the tripod. I couldn't hear his words clearly, as he gestured and smiled at me. He was too cute, and I couldn't stand it. Then he said, "Come by later if you wanna talk about it. The guys should be leaving in an hour or so."

My stomach fluttered as the butterflies slammed into each other. I looked past Jake and noticed Mike was staring at me smugly.

I slowly walked back to my house in a daze, thinking it would be cool if Nadine liked Mike instead. I wished so hard that it would happen. I had a lump in my throat the size of a grapefruit, and my mouth was super dry. Gross, I thought. I went straight to the kitchen and gulped down a glass of water, wondering if anyone else was home.

I shouted out, "Is anyone home?"

There was no response.

The only sound was the whirl of a fan someone forgot to turn off. I was a nervous wreck. I screamed out loud, throwing myself down onto the sofa. I was totally in la-la land. Thank God it was summer time and school wouldn't interfere with whatever was happening. My bag dropped to the floor and I leaned over, taking out Jake's shirt and draped it over my face. I lay on the sofa like that for an hour; peeking out every so often to see how many minutes had ticked by. Finally it was time to check if Jake's band mates were gone. I sprinted up the stairs to my room and stared at myself in the mirror as if my reflection would tell me what to do. I was a mess. Jake was more than *"just Jake"* now.

I ran to my parent's room, the only room in the house that had a view of Jake's backyard and of his bedroom window. When his window blinds were open, there was a clear view into his room, but I didn't see anyone.

I bound down the stairs and slowly opened the front door. I was happy we had a courtyard. No one could see me unless they were standing right in front of the gate. I crept over to the fence nearest Jake's house to see if I could hear anything. There was no longer any muffled music or voices. I pulled over a nearby chair and peeked over the fence to see if see if any of the guy's cars were still parked in front. They were gone.

I walked back into the house with my stomach in knots. I felt silly all of a sudden. Would he think I was a cling-on, a groupie, or whatever they called those fan girls? Finally, after talking to myself forever I made my way to his house.

"Hey," I said softly, approaching his garage.

"Hey, I was just wondering if you were gonna come back over. I was gonna wait a little bit longer and then head over to Dump's house." He flashed his thousand-watt smile at me. My hands began to sweat as my blood rushed to my head. "Are you ok?"

"Yeah, why?"

"I don't know. You look flushed." He looked concerned.

Oh my God! I was totally blushing! What a fucking freak. I had to get a grip! My thoughts smacked against each other as they ran around my brain.

"It's hot out here. Aren't you hot?" I said, fanning my face with my hand. Now I was light-headed.

"Let's go in the house. I'll get you some water."

He grabbed my hand pulling me toward him so he could put his arm around my shoulders. What he didn't realize was when he touched me it made my heart pump faster and my light-headedness even worse. We went into the house and immediately the cold air gave me relief. He sat me at the kitchen counter and handed me water from the fridge. I pressed the cold bottle against my cheek and closed my eyes. I breathed in deeply; telling myself it was no big deal. I could smell the faint scent of him, and I breathed in deeper. Opening my eyes, I felt an instant surge. Jake was still standing there, staring at me. His mouth was slightly open and he was watching me. My insides melted into my feet.

He cleared his throat. "Are you feeling better?"

"Yeah, thanks. I should probably go home and lay down." I got up and stumbled, grabbing the counter. "This sucks, I really wanted to listen to more of your music and…"

"You can lay down on my bed…come on," he interrupted, and grabbed my hand. "You probably just got a little heat stroke or something."

He led me through the house to his room and I thought I was dreaming.

He released my hand and fluffed his pillows. His gesture tugged at my heart even more. "Here, take a load off. Make sure you drink that water."

I collapse on the bed more dramatically than I needed to, but I wanted the smell of him to wrap around me. Just as I sank comfortably into his pillow, another voice came through the house. This time it was a female's.

"Jake?" the voice grew louder.

"Yeah," he shouted, "I'm in my room." He stood up walking to the door and stopped.

"Hey sexy," a raspy voice purred, then a short silence. *"What's going on?"* she asked as she came to the door. By the tone of her voice, it was apparent she'd noticed me lying there. I kept my eyes closed.

"That's my next door neighbor, Alyssa. She's not feeling well, probably from the heat."

"And you couldn't lay her on your couch?"

"Calm down," he said with annoyance.

I could hear their voices fade down the hallway. Then I heard another girl's voice, too. I could barely make out what Jake was saying.

"Look, we were gonna listen to some music, it's no big deal."

"No big deal? Jake, how would you feel if you walked into my room and saw a dude lying on my bed?"

"Rachel, if he was fourteen and your next door neighbor, I wouldn't care."

My stomach dropped. Fourteen, that's what he saw me as - fourteen.

What the hell was I doing? Ok, this happened for a reason. I needed to get a grip. He was way out of my league. He would always be "just Jake," my friend. I sat up and continued listening.

"She's only fourteen," the girl said dryly. *"She doesn't look fourteen."*

"Well, she is. She's gonna be a freshman this year."

"Great." The sarcastic tone continued.

"Look, Rachel, I don't know what else to say."

"You could tell her to go home. We were supposed to be hangin' today."

"Her parents aren't home. I'd feel better if she stayed here until she felt better."

There was long silence and another girl's voice chimed in.

"Rachel, you're outta control. Let's go. Jake, we'll see you later. Don't forget, Dump's expecting you. You might wanna call him."

Then Rachel's voice cut in. *"Call me when she leaves,"* her voice was laced with agitation.

I didn't hear anything else. I took a drink of water and stared at the posters of the hot chicks stuck to his wall. Those are the kind of girls Jake likes. Rachel was probably as hot as those girls hanging on his wall. I laughed to myself, shaking my head.

"Why you shaking your head?" Jake's voice took me by surprise and I jumped.

"I didn't realize I was." I stared back at him sheepishly. "I'm sorry, I didn't mean for you and your girlfriend to fight because of me."

"She's not my girlfriend," he said firmly.

"Sounds like she thinks she is."

"Well, she wants to be, but I don't feel the same way. Besides—"

"So you don't like her?" I interrupted, surprised at my boldness. But I wanted to know. I wanted to know him, every little thing I'd missed after all the time that had gone by.

"Kind of…" He trailed off. Then he laughed. "Only sometimes, after I've had a few beers. No, just kidding. I kinda dig her, yeah, but she's a little hard to handle. She's a spoiled brat, and I don't know if I can deal with that." He sat down next to me.

"What's going on with you, Alyssa?" he probed.

"Well, obviously not too much, since I'm only fourteen." I blurted it out without wanting to, like vomit.

He was silent and I couldn't look at him. I was embarrassed. I could feel him staring at me, burning a hole into the side of my head. I heard him breathe deeply and felt his bed move. He tipped back, lying flat. I glanced over and his hands were over his face, covering his eyes. His shirt came up, exposing his stomach, and all I could do was stare at his smooth skin. I wanted to touch him. He looked through his fingers and caught me staring at him, but I didn't move. Reaching over he touched my arm, tracing it with the tips of his fingers all the way to my hand and held it. I was frozen. My heart raced and tunnel vision took over. The lump in my throat almost choked me. I was worried he'd feel my hand starting to sweat.

"Look, I only said that to calm her down." He let go of my hand and sat up. "Alyssa, you're like family to me. I mean, come on, what's going on here?"

Did he really want to know that this morning he kick-started something in me I'd never felt before? Did *"family"* members do that to each other? I was grossed out at the thought.

"Jake," I said, standing up, "it's nothing. I just felt a little stupid—like I was a kid or something when you said that. I'm not a child. You know, I have feelings too. I'd better go. This was obviously a bad idea, me coming over here and hanging out. I didn't mean to cause problems."

What the hell was I doing? Fuck, I just kept puking all over the place.

"Alyssa, I don't want you to leave, I really want you to stay." He stood up, towering over me. His strong arms embraced me in a hug. "I'm sorry. I didn't mean to hurt your feelings. It was unintentional."

"But I heard you tell Rachel that you'd call her after I left. So she's probably waiting to hear from you soon…"

"Alyssa, I don't wanna see her." He sat down at his desk, facing the screen. "She just rubbed me the wrong way. I'll call her in a little bit to tell her it's a no-go."

He banged at the keys and brought up some music; it filled the air and took the edge off.

He continued to speak. "The cool thing about you is I know where you stand. You were always very open and opinionated, even if the timing was inappropriate." He smiled broadly at me with his perfectly white straight teeth.

"Your teeth are so white," I marveled.

"My mom makes me use those white strips," he said, rolling his eyes.

"Well, it makes you that much more *sexy*," I said, laughing at myself for emphasizing the word "sexy" with hand quotations. Jake's face bent with amusement. "I'm sorry, I shouldn't make fun."

He shook his head. "A little fire in you, I see. I can never underestimate you, can I?"

6

ALYSSA

Jake and I sat in his room for hours, talking about music and his past tours. When I expressed interest in playing the guitar, he insisted on teaching me. When I finally looked over at the clock, it was 5:30 PM.

"Shit, the time!" I panicked. "Um, I should probably get going. I left my phone at home in my bag. The units are probably wondering where I'm at."

"Shit! And I forgot to call Rachel. Great. She's really gonna be happy now. Guess we're both in trouble, huh?" He slumped. "Now, don't get pissed, but I don't wanna hear it from her, so I'm not gonna tell her you stayed here the whole time. It's just easier."

He walked out of the room. I could hear his voice, but couldn't decipher his words with the music playing in the background. Then his voice grew louder. Were they fighting? I wanted to know more about this Rachel. I was going to ask my sister if she knew her and break out the yearbook so I could see what she looked like. Staring at the snapshots with the two girls again, I wondered which one she was.

Jake walked back in agitated. He threw his phone hard at the bed.

"You know, it's probably better it happened like this." He shut his door. He stood there shaking his head "Fuck, what a bitch. Oh, by the way, my mom's home now. I don't need her poking around here, that's why I shut the door."

"Why's your mom's a bitch?" I asked, shocked.

"No! Duh, Rachel." He plopped onto the bed. "She's too much. I'm glad it's out in the open, how lame she is. No matter what I told her, she still thought you were here."

"Well, I was…am…you know what they say about women's intuition."

He lifted his head from the pillow and leered at me. "Don't be a smartass. It's not like she's my girlfriend. She's been my friend for a long time and helps out with the band stuff a lot. We hang, but it's not like we're together."

"So, you don't think you could be leading her on? I mean, sorry to point it out, but you kinda acted like you cared when she came over earlier. You know, making excuses and trying to make her feel better about me being here."

His arms fell heavy against the mattress. "I see why she would think I like her like that, then. I mean I do, but not like that. That was a long time ago, when I thought I was interested." He sighed deeply, "Then with her freaking out about you and acting all territorial n'shit? I mean, she doesn't even fucking know you!" He gestured his hand at me. "She's lame."

"Tell her to beat it, then."

"Yeah, right. It's not gonna be that easy."

I looked out the back door and walked over to it. I stared at the far end of the backyard and wondered if the gate still worked. My dad had installed a gate so we could easily go from yard to yard when we were younger.

"Hey, is that gate still working?" I walked out the door. There were a couple of palm trees and other plants that blocked the path.

"I'm sure it does. We didn't do anything to it. I forgot it was there." He walked in front of me, rooting through the palms and unlatched it. He struggled with it a bit, and it finally opened.

"Yay!" I cheered and Jake raised his hand for me to give him a high-five. I squeezed through and was wedged against him for a moment. I felt that shock again when we touched and I loved it.

"Well, this is gonna make things interesting," he whispered.

What was that supposed to mean? My head spun. I turned back and hugged him. I couldn't help myself.

"Jake, thanks so much, fun times." I took in a deep breath through my nose to smell him one last time. His face pressed against my hair and neck. I could have stayed frozen there forever.

"Mmm, you smell good. Your hair smells like strawberries." He let me go and I almost passed out after hearing his words.

"I was just thinking the same thing. You smell good too. I'll talk to you later," I whispered loudly. I was numb from my excitement.

"Hey, if you're not doing anything later, you wanna come back and watch a movie?"

"Sure, if I'm not in trouble for something." I waved goodbye. "Probably sometime after nine."

I opened the back door and my mom smiled. "Well, hello." She came out from behind the counter to hug me, and then grabbed my shoulders, holding me at arm's length. "You have a nice glow. What have you been up to?"

She went back to chopping veggies. My dad brushed by me with a beer in hand without a word.

"Hi, Dad," I waved with false excitement.

"Hello, my dear." He collapsed into his chair and turned on the TV. That was the extent of our relationship.

"I've actually been hanging out with Jake today." I beamed.

"Is that right? And what's Jake been up to these days?" my mom asked, carefully placing each foil-wrapped potato in the oven.

"You know he has a band, right?" I said. "He practices every day, you must hear it."

"Yes, I hear it on the weekends. I suppose he plays before we get home from work." She turned, grabbing a bottle of red wine, filling her glass. I wondered what wine tasted like. I remembered Jake saying that he drank beer. I hadn't tasted any alcohol yet.

"Mom, can I have a taste of that? I'm just curious what the big deal is. I mean, you drink it every night."

With a wary eye, she handed her glass to me without saying a word. I smelled it, took a sip, and gagged. "Uh, thanks but no thanks. It's like fire going down my throat. Why do you drink that?"

I walked to the sink, sticking my mouth under the faucet.

"I drink because I like it; it's an acquired taste. All wines taste differently. It relaxes me after a long day of work, and it's good for my heart. That is why I drink it, in moderation."

"Including moderation itself," my father weaseled in. My mom rolled her eyes.

"What does beer taste like, then? I hate the smell of beer."

"I don't like it either. Go ask your father for a sip. Frank, give Aly a sip of your beer, she's curious."

My father held up the bottle of beer over his head, without a word, no fight, nothing. I walked over and took a sip just as my brother rounded the corner coming down the stairs.

"What, you let her drink, but not me?" he grabbed the beer from my hand and took a long swig.

"Goddammit, Kyle!" my father roared. "We know what you get into, give it back to her."

"Geez, calm down, sorry." He wiped his mouth with the back of his hand, handing me the beer. His eyes were wide. I stuck my tongue out at him and he flipped me off. "What's she doin' with it then?"

"She's not drinking, Kyle," Mom explained. "She's tasting, she was curious."

"Yeah, and I'm a girl," he guffawed. "I'm calling her bullshit."

I handed the beer back to my father and turned, punching my brother right in the gut.

"Ok, you two," my mom said dryly. "Stop it."

"What, you're not gonna punish her? If I woulda' done that, you woulda' grounded me!"

"Kyle, that's enough," my dad growled. "We were having a nice moment and you come down here, stirring the pot."

Kyle glared at me.

"Kyle, I swear I've never had one drink," I assured him.

He looked at me cautiously. "Whatever," he said under his breath, and mouthed *BEEEAAATCH* to my face. I flipped him off in return.

"What's for dinner?" he asked, shoving me out of the way as he passed into the kitchen. He opened the fridge and rummaged around.

"Close the door, Kyle. I'm making artichoke dip, and we're having steak and baked potatoes."

She poured a bag of corn chips into a bowl. Kyle walked over, took a handful and stuffed a few in his mouth. *What a pig*, I thought. I took stock of Kyle. Sure, he was cute, for being my brother. No wonder he and Jake grew apart; he'd become a total polo shirt-wearing nerd. A pang of guilt came over me for thinking that, but he was, plain and simple. One day he would find a nerd girl to share his nerd life with.

We sat down to eat, and my sister barely said a word. She was attached to her phone throughout dinner, like always. Which reminded me—I never called Nicole. "Mom, anyone, did I get any calls?" I looked around the table.

Finally Allison looked up as she took another bite of food, "No, but your chicks came over looking for you, and your phone kept ringing. Where were you anyway?"

"I was next door at Jake's. He was teaching me to play the guitar and we were talking about his music."

I said all those words on purpose. I wanted Allison to know. In my own way, I wanted to feel like I was one-upping her. I could feel her staring at me and didn't want to look at her. I looked at Kyle instead, but he was concentrating on his food and Mom and Dad were talking quietly. I finally looked at Allison and just as I thought, she was staring at me with an obtuse grin. You see, about a year prior she used to have the hots for Jake, until she got another guy to like her.

"Really, is that right?" Allison's condescending tone rang through my ears.

I didn't want to stare at her. She would see right through me and try to knock me down. Nope, I was going to eat my dinner, wait for everyone to go to sleep. Then I was gonna to go back over to Jake's house via the secret route and watch movies with him. No one would know. After 9 PM my mom and dad would be locked in their room. Kyle would be gone like usual, and who knows what Allison would be into. I was always locked away in my room after 9 PM, or at Nicole's house.

"Can I be excused?" I said loudly.

"Sure," My father said, glancing back at my mother.

I grabbed my plate and walked into the kitchen. I heard Allison ask to be excused too and I rushed to rinse my plate. I wanted to leave before she got into the kitchen, but it was no good. I felt her standing behind me.

"So, Aly. Tell me about Jake."

"What's to tell? You know what he's been into, right?" I didn't want to come off as too cocky, but I couldn't' help myself.

"Yeah, but he never asked me to hang out at his house and listen to his music, or teach me to play the guitar."

She wanted dirt, but I wouldn't budge. I would never let her know how I felt about Jake.

"Well, did you ask him to teach you to play the guitar?" I could feel her eyes raking me up and down.

"Uh…no." Her sarcastic tone returned. "Did you?"

"Not exactly, I only said it's something I've wanted to learn, and he offered."

"Oh, I see. I'm sure he felt obligated."

I really hated how she treated me, and I was glad she was jealous. Moments went by. I continued to do the dishes, hoping she would leave, because I was running out of dishes to wash.

"You wanna hand me your plate?"

"You know, Aly, you better be careful," her tone changed. It almost sounded like she cared. "Boys like Jake only want one thing, and a freshie like you is just what's on the menu."

My stomach sank. What was she saying? I thought of all the stories Greg would tell us late at night in Nicole's backyard about his brothers hooking up with chicks. It made my stomach turn. But I couldn't talk to Allison. She wasn't trustworthy. She would sell me out to our parents for sure.

"What's that supposed to mean?" I glared at her. My hand dropped to my side, dripping water onto the floor. She made me sick. What kind of sister would really be jealous of her younger sibling? But it was always that way. She would always try to be the best, to outshine me…to be a bitch.

She sighed, hedging on her words, choosing carefully what she would say next. Then she looked me in the eyes. "Aly, I'm serious. I'm not trying to be the mean big sister. Guys like Jake only want one thing, and once they get it, its dump city. There are other things you need to be concerned with, too, so just be careful."

I was finally alone in the kitchen. I looked at the clock. 8 PM. I went to the couch to get my bag and noticed Jake's shirt lying there. I picked it up and stuffed it back in my bag before digging for my phone. I dialed Nicole's number.

"Hey, it's me," I whispered. I dreaded talking to her.

"Where the hell have you been? We've been waiting for you all day. Nadine is freaking out. We hung out on the corner, waiting for you to show up. Jake never came out of his house. We knocked on your door at 4, and your sister said you weren't home."

"I was home, sleeping. I didn't feel well." I didn't want to lie, but I felt like I had to. I wanted to tell her, but I just couldn't.

"Oh, I'm sorry. Are you feeling better?"

"Yeah, I'm fine now. I think it's just the heat."

"Okay, are you coming over tomorrow? Matt's gonna be home, so you know he'll be over here."

This perked my interest. "Yeah, I'll be over."

"Ok, see you tomorrow. Oh, and call Nadine, she's comin' outta her skin to know what went down with Jake."

"Sure. See ya tomorrow." I hung up the phone, unsure of what to feel. Matt was going to be home. Normally, I would be excited. But I only thought of Jake and watched the minutes tick by as I waited for my parents to tuck in.

I decided to take a shower. I normally took showers in the morning, but since I was going to Jake's, I wanted to feel good. As I got ready for my night, I reasoned with myself…Why should this be any different than all the other times Jake and I watched movies together? Yeah right, whom was I kidding? I liked him now; that was the difference. This wasn't the same—at least not for me.

9 PM rolled around quicker than I wanted it to. I was nervous. I heard my parents disappear into their bedroom. I brushed my damp hair and went into the bathroom to brush my teeth. My sister was just getting out of the shower.

"What are you doing tonight?" I asked, trying to sound casual.

"Like you care?" She sniffed.

Why did she have to be so lame? Kyle was gone, thank God. Back in my room I closed the door behind me. I stared at myself in the mirror once more. I wore black cotton shorts and a black tank top. Simple but flattering enough, I thought. I put on lip-gloss and I stared at my chest. I pulled down my tank top a little lower, just like Nadine did. Ugh, what was I doing? There was no way I'd ever look that big unless I got a boob job—and that certainly wasn't going to happen.

I heard my sister shut her door and she immediately started talking loudly. I turned off my light and turned on my TV. I messed up my bed and gently shut my door, making my way down the stairs and out into the warm night air.

Jake must have heard me struggling with the gate, because he was standing at the door, waiting for me. I felt like I was dreaming.

7

JAKE

When I watched Aly go back into her house while I hid at our "secret entrance," it really started to hit me that she was unlike any of the girls I knew. I dug her—completely. Making my way back into my room I sat in front of my computer and opened my email. I glanced over the messages Rachel told me about. More dates for local shows before we were to leave on tour. I wasn't sure if we could pull any of them off. I brought up my calendar in attempt to figure out the timing of everything, but my mood was strange.

I felt empty inside and I couldn't focus. I knew right away it was because of Alyssa. Liking her was the last thing I needed. I didn't need any distractions in my life. The thing with Rachel was gonna be enough for me to handle, but there I sat, wondering if *Aly* was really going to come back.

I wasn't in the mood to work. I lay on my bed and watched the time tick by before finally turning on the TV, which did nothing to distract me from my thoughts of her. I should have gotten her phone number. What if her parents caught her sneaking out? I wondered if she really had the balls to go through with it. Who knew what girls tried to get away with at that age? Ugh, that was another thing—her age.

As always, my acoustic guitar came to my rescue. It stared at me from the corner of my room, perched perfectly in its stand, calling to me. Grabbing it, I sat on my bed, tracing my fingers across its smooth wooden contours. I thought about Rachel and Aly, comparing them to each other. Thoughts flooded my brain and I grew anxious. I felt bad about Rachel, regardless of her personality flaws. I told myself not to waste my time worrying about her. What would be would be. My mind twisted back to Aly, and thoughts began to get the best of me. I wondered what it would mean if she *did* show up. I thought about how soft she felt when I hugged her at the gate, and the way her hair smelled. I liked how clean she was. She wasn't sticky and made up like all the others.

I pictured Aly creeping down the stairs, out of her house, and into my room. For a brief second I wondered if she'd want to make out. I quickly pushed it from my mind, reminding myself what she was to me. She was my kid next-door neighbor, or at least she used to be; the few years' age difference shouldn't matter now. Besides, I told myself, she probably wouldn't show.

I began to strum a tune and the words began to flow—grabbing a pad of paper, I had the whole song written in less than an hour:

TRANSPOSE

Sleepless nights aren't new to me
All these thoughts are killing me
Someone come and put me to ease
All of my anxiety
There's no cause that I can see
What's this scratching at my brain

And I can't stop
even if I wanted to
It's up top
Maybe I'm simply deluded
That's right
Here I am just wasting my time
All my time
And it's hard to justify what you can do
I'm so sick and tired of falling through
It's true, maybe I've been wasting my time
All this time

Come creeping, no one can hear you now
I listen, so you can show me how
There's something that I'm missing here
Softly, stab my evil dreams
Faster, help me fall asleep
Come close, I don't wanna see you again

From time to time, we fall in line
But now it seems that we are blind
No one knows, that's how it goes
all the thoughts that we transpose

And I can't stop
even if I wanted to

It's up top
Maybe I'm simply deluded
That's right
Here I am just wasting my time
All my time
And It's hard to justify what you can do
I'm so sick and tired of falling through
It's true, Maybe I've been wasting my time
All this time

Just as I hit the last chord, I heard the gate make noise, at exactly the same moment my phone began to ring. It was Notting. My heart sprung up into my throat. She fucking showed. Now what? I had to take Notting's call and answered the phone. I would have to tell him I would call him back. What the hell was I getting myself into?

Smiling to myself, I realized that I didn't even care.

Enjoy this excerpt from

FIRST KISS
Book 1

1

JAKE

I could still feel the warmth from her body on the sheets when I reached over, searching for her, and for a moment I wondered…had it been real? Bleary-eyed, I stared at the clock. It was only 7 in the morning. The sound that woke me must have been the door shutting— Aly sneaking away. We must have fallen asleep sometime after midnight.

She shouldn't have stayed over. She'd kept trying to leave, but I'd keep pulling her back into the bed. Not that anything had happened. We'd just talked and hung all over each other, horsing around. Kid shit. I sighed, rubbing my eyes as I sat back down on the edge of the bed. What did I expect? She *was* a kid. Alyssa Montgomery. What the hell was I doing, hanging with a girl her age? If her parents caught her sneaking back in this morning…

I swore and tripped on the sheet tangled around my leg as I hopped from the bed. I opened the door to the backyard to see if she was still visible, but I was too late. It was quiet and cool. I shivered, standing there, wondering when I'd see her again. As I reached for my phone, I saw that three texts had come through. They were all from Rachel Schaffer.

I didn't read them—I just tossed my phone to the foot of my bed. I seriously didn't even wanna deal with that shit right now. One drunken hook-up and what, she thought she had dibs on me? Yeah, she was an old friend, and she helped out with our band stuff...but I'd seen how she plays hot and cold with other guys; she should know what's up. And it's not like I'd ever shown even the slightest interest in her. But still, I just *knew* that it was gonna rain shit-balls once she realized that I was into Aly. I pushed the looming issue from my mind and tried to go back to sleep. This was my last summer vacation, and I wanted to go into my senior year with my future in music secure.

I could smell Aly's strawberry-scented hair lingering on my pillow and closed my eyes, reliving our night. When she'd first arrived, I'd sat down on my bed while she paced back and forth in front of me. I recalled how she looked in her little black cotton shorts. Her long legs were tan and smooth. It'd taken everything in me not to reach out and touch them. When I finally did, I think she had the softest skin I'd ever felt on a girl.

I guess I finally drifted off to sleep, because I was startled awake by a knock at my door.

"Yeah, what?" I groaned.

"Rachel is here. It's eleven o'clock," my mom's muffled voice informed me.

Shit. Are you kidding me? "Alright, tell her to come in." I threw off the blankets, sat up, and before I knew it Rachel was standing there, glaring at me.

"What's up, man? What's so important that you had to wake me up?" I stood, grabbing a shirt off the back of my chair and pulled it on.

"Really? Man?" she huffed, shoulders slumping.

"Dude, what is up with you?"

"Me? What about you?"

"Are you kidding me, Rachel? I was up all night…writing." I turned, holding my arms out, pleading. "Come on. What's up? What's this all about?"

"You totally blew me off, Jake. You fuck around with me, and then you ignore me?"

"Ok, wait a second." I scoffed. "I could say the same thing about you. You fucked around with me too, Rachel."

I knew trying to put it on her was a dick move, but I didn't even care. I'd had enough of it.

"Yeah, but I'm not blowing you off."

I stood there, mind racing to find something to smooth over our exchange.

"Look, I don't mean to blow you off. Come on, I'm just doin' my thing. You have no idea the shit that's about to go down—I have to focus."

She stood silent as her eyes searched me up and down, then they roamed around my room. Slowly, she began to walk around, searching as if she finally sensed that someone else had been there. My stomach sank. I could still smell Aly's scent on me, and Rachel could probably smell it too. I backed away and went into the bathroom, turning on the water. I rinsed my face. I didn't want to deal with the drama of it all. I walked out, drying my face as I waited for her to say something.

We stood there, silently staring at each other. She was trying to read me. I didn't know what to say.

She broke the silence first.

"I don't want things to change, Jake." Her voice was void of her usual bitchy tone, which only made it harder. It'd have been easier to ignore her if she was being her usual overdramatic self.

"Rachel, nothing's gonna change if we just move past what happened."

"What am I supposed to do with that?"

She moved close to me, taking my hand. Her fake nails raked against my palm. I looked down at her perfectly painted red lips and could only think of Aly. I laughed at the absurdity of the moment, gently pulling my hand away from hers and grabbing her shoulder.

"We're gonna chalk up that blurred night to something that just happened and chill. I don't want things to change."

"Then don't ignore me," she said, standing on her tiptoes trying to kiss me. I turned my head away, and she stiffened.

I could hear her breath escape her.

I backed away. "Rachel, I'm sorry. I have a million things on my mind, and it's got nothing to do with you."

Her eyes flashed with disappointment. I waited for her to berate me, but she surprised me once again with silence. Sadly, I knew it would never be the same between us and it was only gonna get worse.

"I'm sorry, too," she said quietly and kept looking around my room, walking toward my bed. Panic filled me. My eyes dashed around the bed and floor, looking for any trace of Aly. I didn't see anything.

"Look, Rachel, I don't' mean to blow you off, but I gotta meet with Notting. Apparently we got some sort of a licensing deal for a movie or something."

Her eyes lit up. "Wow, that's awesome. Which one? What's it all about?"

"I don't know anything yet," I said, maybe a little too harshly.

"Geez. Ok. Grumpy." She shook her head. "I'll just talk to you later then. Um, and just ignore those text messages. You obviously didn't read them yet."

"Yeah, ok," I replied, grabbing the back of my neck and rubbing it. The tension was giving me a headache.

"Is there anything I can do to help?"

"No, Rachel, there isn't." I sighed deeply, deciding just to lay my thoughts out there. "Don't worry about helping with anything right now. I don't have it in me to deal with it. Just chill, ok?"

I could see her swallow.

"Alright, then," she replied, obviously trying to play it cool. "Whatever. I guess call me later. Or not."

She left with her sarcasm hovering over me. I just stood there, unable to say anything. I felt like a jerk. It was weird seeing her like this; all vulnerable and unsure of herself. I pushed it from my mind.

It seemed that every other thought throughout the afternoon was about Aly. I sat talking with Notting, my manager and father figure, and tried to focus on what he was saying. A production company had commissioned us to write an original score. Even though the movie was a low-budget flick, it had some well-known actors attached. I was stoked. After Notting left, the guys and I sat around the garage, tinkering with our instruments. I got up and hit the switch to open the door.

"Dude, it's fucking hot out there—you're gonna let all the cold air out," Mike whined. I ignore him.

"What are you doing?" Bobby chimed.

"I'll close it in a sec." I said, and walked out to my truck pretending to look for something. I glanced over at Aly's house, hoping she'd miraculously appear. I didn't have her phone number and wondered if she'd surprise me by coming back over later. I thought back to our conversation the night before.

"You don't think this is weird?" She'd asked in a whisper.

"Don't be silly. We're just watching a movie."

Our legs pressed against each other's, and I recalled how hard it had been not to be all over her. I wanted it to be chill—but it was far from that for me.

"It's nice to have someone different to hang with, you know," she said quietly. "And it's cool that you're next door."

"Yeah. If you see lights, come over anytime."

"Really?"

"Yeah, sure."

I thought about how the light from the TV had made her eyes sparkle as she'd smiled, clasping her hands, pressing them under her chin before she rolled over onto her side. Her reaction was so endearing it pulled me in even more. With her back facing me, I pictured myself running my hand gently over her arm, down to her side. I wanted to touch her legs so bad. Just thinking about it made me tug at my pants.

I hoped she'd take what I said to heart and come over later.

Dump's drumming and Bobby's baseline pulled me back to reality.

"Hey, that sounds good," I shouted over the music. "Start over."

I needed to focus on the music.

Over the next hour we hashed out something pretty clever for the film, though I was so distracted that my shit was rough around the edges. Dump and Bobby's parts were solid. Mike would draft off me when I was finished. But no matter what the other guys did, my mind kept drifting back to the song I'd written the night before about Aly as I'd waited for her to sneak over. It'd come easier than any song I'd ever written before—like magic. There was something about that girl...

Finally, I gathered the courage to say something. "So I wrote a new song the other night and it's a little different, kinda, and I wanna know what you think."

"Shoot," Dump encouraged.

I took a deep breath and began. I couldn't look any of them in the faces for the entire song. After it was over though, I looked up, steeling myself for their reactions. Bobby wore a huge grin. Dump nodded his head and tucked his tatted arms to his chest. Mike's mouth hung open.

"Interesting lyrics, where'd you pull those from?" Mike remarked.

Again, I ignored him. No one else said anything.

"So?" I asked. "Any other commentary?"

"Nope. I dig it," Bobby approved.

Dump still sat there, nodding his head with his eyes closed. "I'm bumpin' some shit around. All right. It's a little lighter, but I gotcha. The lyrics are cool."

I smiled, satisfied.

Later on, I sat at my computer watching random YouTube videos. The day had flown by; it was already

8:15 PM. The bright light from my computer screen cut through the gray haze of fading sunlight that consumed my room and reminded me to turn on the lights. The code now set. Would Aly remember that I told her if she saw my lights on to come over anytime? I got up and opened my back door.

A rush of adrenaline coursed through me when I heard the faint rattle of the gate outside in the distance. I jumped up, going to the door, wondering if I was hearing things. Euphoria overcame me when I saw Aly's darkened figure come through the bushes.

With a grin, I stepped out to meet her.

2

ALYSSA

I must have been hallucinating, because he looked like he was glowing, backlit from the lights behind him. He didn't have a shirt on and his broad shoulders dominated my vision. I didn't know what to say other than "*Hey*". He winked at me and I felt that intense electric surge when I brushed past him into his room. He stood in silence, and a smile spread broad across his face.

"I was wondering when you'd wanna hang again." He beamed, and my mouth went dry.

"Yeah, I was wondering if you'd mind. So I thought what the heck, I'd see." I shrugged and sat down on his bed, waving around the movie cases I held. I'd taken them from my brother. He and Jake used to be best friends years ago and would certainly have a lot to say if he knew where I was. "I borrowed these from Kyle."

Jake came and sat down next to me, grabbing the movies out of my hand. I went numb. *Really though, what the hell was I doing here?* I couldn't take all the questions bouncing around in my head. I'd barely eaten anything since the night before. I concluded I had to ask him about his relationship with that girl Rachel 'cause it was eating at me big time, not to mention the feelings that swarmed through me. Yesterday, when I'd first gone to his room, she'd come by and caught a glimpse of me lying on his bed. He made innocent excuses when she gave him a hard time about it. It was obvious that there was *something* between them…but what? My gut was telling me that there was more to them than just her crushing on him, as he made it out to be. Oddly enough, I wasn't nervous about our impending talk. I would still be his friend no matter what his response. I would still want to come and talk music, and have him teach me to play the guitar. At least, that's what I told myself, but with those thoughts, the truth came fast behind. I also didn't want to think something was happening between us if it was only happening in my head.

I kept thinking about poor Matt Squire. He had been my main crush for so long, and now Jake? Matt would be returning from Vegas the next day, and I wondered what I would feel for him now. I was completely and utterly confused. Or was I? All I knew was that I loved the way Jake made me feel.

I was fidgety, and Jake immediately called me out on my mood. He reached over and grabbed my hand and I froze. I wanted to curl my fingers around his, but I stopped myself. I didn't know which way was up. Finally, he spoke again lightening the mood, and our conversation drifted to the new song he'd written. I begged him to play it for me, and when he did I wanted to die. The way he looked, sitting there strumming his guitar without his shirt on, left me speechless. Everything about him was perfect. He was so talented. When our small talk ended, I decided to go for it.

My stomach did cartwheels.

"Jake, I have a question." I breathed deeply, trying not to hyperventilate. "I'm just going to ask, because I don't know how else to do it." I paused for a long moment. Our eyes were locked.

His cheerful expression turned to concern at the seriousness of my tone. He froze, speaking slowly. "Okay."

My heart raced.

I paced back and forth what seemed like a million times. Finally, Jake grabbed me by the waist and drew me onto his lap. When he touched me it felt like I was plugged into an electrical socket. He held me snug, placing his chin on my shoulder and spoke softly into my ear. His tone was measured. I thought I was going to faint. My heart raced and my hands started to sweat, again and I gulped for air.

"What's up? Something's obviously on your mind."

I closed my eyes. "Do you feel it?" I breathed heavily.

"What? Feel what?" he asked, holding his breath, in an attempt to feel *it*.

"The electricity or whatever it is," I tried to explain. I held my breath too, wanting it to last.

"The electricity," he repeated slowly. He moved me off his lap, but my legs remained draped across his thighs. "What are you talking about?"

I was instantly mortified. "Never mind. I'm just going crazy, that's all. This was a bad idea."

I knew it was only I feeling anything at all—whom was I kidding, anyway? I was just a stupid girl with a stupid crush. I was embarrassed, and I deserved it. I threw myself back onto his pillows.

"Hey, don't stop," he said softly. "I wanna understand."

Holy crap. What else did I have to lose? I'd already completely embarrassed myself. He could take this back to his stupid friends and have a laugh. I covered my eyes with both hands, wanting to rip my eyes out of my head. I breathed in deeply, trying to come up with something to say, and kept peeking out between my fingers. The seconds ticked by and Jake stared at me tenderly, shaking my knee. My words came out like a bursting dam.

"Jake, when I get near you, it's this feeling I've never felt before. I'm embarrassed to admit it, but the only way I can describe it is, electricity. It's like this weird energy that passes from you to me." I wouldn't look at him. A long moment passed and his cell phone began to ring. "Now I feel stupid," I blurted out. Thankfully he ignored the call.

"Don't feel stupid." His voice soothed my frayed nerves. He sat quietly, contemplating his next words, nodding his head. He placed his hands on my thighs and I seriously thought I would die. I still wouldn't look at him for any longer than a second. "I guess that's the way you could describe or explain it. It's also known as sexual tension," he said flatly. My stomach dropped. So he thinks I've already had sex? I was shocked. What the hell? The shift of my emotions was too much, and they ran up my spine and out of my mouth.

"I've never done that!" I spat, jumping up. "I've never even really kissed a boy!" I wanted him to know I wasn't some slut. There were girls my age who were already known for hooking up with guys, their reputations tarnished by their easy, teasing ways.

"Alyssa, calm down, that's not what I'm saying. It's just another way to describe the energy that flows between the opposite sex when they're attracted to each other," he explained. "It's also known as chemistry."

My warning bells were going off as I remembered what my sister, Allison, had said to me just the night before: "*Guys like Jake only want one thing, and when they get it, it's dump city.*"

Jake was gonna try and get in my pants, wasn't he? I started to panic.

"I should probably go." I tried to walk past him, but he grabbed my arm and I flinched, blurting out, "You're not gonna try to have sex with me, are you?" I pressed my eyes tightly closed. I wanted to cry, feeling the sting in my eyes and the burn in my nose.

Jake laughed nervously and immediately let go of my arm.

"Whoa, whoa, no, absolutely not. I wouldn't just take that away from you." He paused. "Or force you to do that."

His face maintained a serious expression, his eyes searching mine.

A few silent seconds passed. My brain fought to catch up, deciphering his words. "Take what away?" I asked, not immediately understanding what he meant.

"Your, your," he stuttered and paced around. He grabbed the top of his head and looked at the ceiling. "Whoa, warp speed, all in a day. I guess we're making up for lost time."

He forced a smile, but didn't look happy.

"Jake, I'm sorry, I didn't mean to…"

"Alyssa, don't be sorry." He shook his head. "Let me explain something to you. Guys and girls, sometimes this is how it goes." He gestured between us.

We stared at each other for a long moment until something came to my mind.

"Like love at first sight?" I couldn't help myself. I sounded so naïve.

"I'm not sure about that, to be honest. But I can tell you that you're not misreading anything. There's something here."

"So, you've felt this with someone before?" I asked, even though I knew what the answer would be and didn't want to hear it.

"Yes, I have."

I was disappointed. *There goes my schoolgirl dream of finding true love—of being the one.* It was ridiculous, and I knew it.

"You have." I confirmed. My voice was barely audible.

"Take Rachel for example. I was attracted to her at first, but then after I got to know her and what she was really like, that feeling vanished into thin air, like it was never there."

"But you don't feel it with me. It's just a one-way thing, then," I stated. I was exhausted from my emotions.

I plopped over onto the bed, rolling onto my side to face him. He was so perfect and I was so foolish. To think I was anything special was idiotic. I pushed his pillow under my head and closed my eyes, breathing in his scent again. I swear, I'd never get enough of the way he smelled. When I opened my eyes, he was staring at me curiously from across the room. I mustered a little smile and croaked out a question.

"Do you want me to leave, Jake?"

"No, I want you to stay, if you wanna stay." There was sincerity in his voice. He turned around, fiddling with the DVD player, and started the movie over again. I wondered briefly about his mom. I never saw her anymore.

The next thing I knew, Jake hopped in bed behind me and stuffed a pillow under his head. I was paralyzed. I could feel the heat radiating from his body even though he wasn't touching me. The sensation was electrifying. I was completely captivated by the way I felt when I was around him. The peaks and valleys of everything he exuded enamored me. It was there, that *tension* again. I could feel his breath on my shoulder. I flinched as he moved my hair away from my neck.

"I'm sorry," he whispered. His hand moved down my arm, giving me the chills. He tucked his arm around my waist, pulling me closer to him. My heart skipped a beat. I could feel his breathing speed up, too. "Alyssa, let's just not read into this whole thing. I *do* feel what you feel. I enjoy being here with you, and that's the way it is."

"I'm-"

"And I'm not going to do anything that would ever hurt you," he interrupted. "You can trust me on that. I promise." He squeezed me tight. I could feel him burying his face in the nape of my neck, and it gave me butterflies. His promise echoed in my head, mingling with the butterflies fluttering around every inch of me, lulling me to sleep.

***

I was dreaming the most awesome dream; I was still in Jake's bed and my head lay on his chest. He had me safely tucked under his arm. My consciousness returned, jolting me awake. It wasn't a dream at all. I sat up in a near panic, thinking about my parents. I was lying with

Jake and he *was* holding me. Dawn was barely shining and the clock read 6:12 AM. Jake's eyes fluttered open at my movement. His dark lashes framed his bright blue eyes, mesmerizing me. I wanted to stay right there, forever, staring at his face. He squinted at me, smiling softly.

"Shit, we're no joke with that sleep," he said, sitting up. Still shirtless, his hair was all mussed. He looked amazing for just having woken up. I wondered what I looked like. I walked to the mirror, attempting to brush my hair with my fingers, and I immediately got self-conscious.

"Do you have to leave?" he asked, grabbing a thick comforter at the foot of the bed. We had only slept with a thin blanket and the warmth of the night, and now a morning chill had consumed the room from leaving the back door open.

"No, I can't go home yet, my parents are up getting ready for work. They're probably in the kitchen, drinking coffee." I laughed. "Yeah, hey mom, hey dad…I was just sleeping in Jake's bed."

He flashed a lop-sided smile. "Come lie back down then. Go back to sleep. It's too early," he said, slapping the pillow next to him.

I crawled back in next to him. There was no way I was going back to sleep, not lying there so close to him. He held me just like he did during the night. I started to daydream about what it would be like to have Jake as a boyfriend. We would be going to school together soon. He would be able to drive me, and I wouldn't have to depend on my brother or sister.

I could see us pulling in the parking lot together and him putting his arm around my shoulder as we walked across campus. Wouldn't that be a dream? I was crazy to think it would ever happen; my father would never allow it. And of course, there was Rachel and the rest of The Envies. Now *that* was reality, I thought as I closed my eyes, hoping ninth grade would be easy.

"You know," I mused, "technically these aren't the first times we've stayed together. We can just add this sleepover to all the others."

"Nope, we've done this a million times. But this is the first time we've been at my house, and we're teenagers. Not sure our parents would agree."

"Oh sure they would, no big deal right? If I get caught, I'll just act stupid. "*Oh, mom, dad, I didn't think you'd care, we used to have sleepovers all the time.*"

"Aly," he said firmly, squeezing my waist. "Zip it, go back to sleep." His voice was tired and raspy.

"I'm sorry." I whispered. I lay there wide-awake, feeling his breath get heavier on my shoulder. He fell back to sleep.

I must have fallen back to sleep quickly enough, too, because I couldn't recall any more of my daydream. Now it was 9 AM and Jake was standing in front of the TV brushing his teeth, still shirtless. I marveled at him and immediately got up. I was wishing I had someone to share my fabulous night with, but I was alone in my deeds.

"Ok, I gotta go," I announced, standing by the door. He turned around smiling, mouth full of toothpaste.

"Hold on," he mumbled. I could hear the water in the bathroom turn on. He was back in no time, opening a drawer and pulling out a t-shirt, tragically covering his brilliant naked torso. I smirked without realizing it.

"What?" he asked half laughing.

"Oh, nothing," I giggled. "It's nothing. I'm just laughing at myself."

He smiled, opening his back door, walking out into the cool morning air. He shivered, crossing his arms to his chest. We looked over and up at my house. Everything was still and quiet, with the exception of the sound of cars whizzing by in the distance. It was sunny and bright already. A cool ocean breeze whipped my hair in my face. He reached over and brushed it out of my eyes. His touch sent bolts of lightning through me.

"See ya later," he said.

Was that a question or a statement?

"Yeah," I mumbled, smiling weakly, not sure what else to say. I went through the gate, heart pounding, wondering if someone would see me come from Jake's yard. I reminded myself that I needed to act normal. I needed to get ready for my day and meet everyone as I always had. Nadine would be waiting anxiously. Matt would be there, too. I wondered how I would feel about Matt when I saw him later and anxiety filled me at the thought.

I had unlocked the office door before I left just in case the slider got locked and it was. I crept in, looking around quickly. Standing still, I held my breath. I didn't hear anything but the faint sound of a TV. I strolled down the hall toward the kitchen, where our family portraits stared at me accusingly. My brother was on the sofa watching TV. He didn't even acknowledge my presence. This was good. I poured some orange juice and walked upstairs. My sister's door was closed. She was probably still sleeping. Once again, no one noticed that I'd been gone the whole night. I was giddy with excitement.

I stared at myself in my bedroom mirror, and for the next couple of hours I was lost in the haze of Jake. I finally returned Nadine's text messages from the day before, telling her to meet me. I was sure everyone would notice me glowing like a light bulb. How was I gonna keep a lid on this? The fact that Nadine noticed Jake first and made it known that she wanted him had me reeling. I was sneaking around, behind my best friend's back, professing deep like for Jake to his face.

I was sick at the thought of it. How was I to know that I'd be overpowered by the chemistry Jake spoke of? I quickly picked out a new bathing suit, a shredded jean mini-skirt and white tank. I smelled my shoulders, and they smelled like him. I didn't want to shower. I wanted to smell like him all day long.

3

ALYSSA

I sat on Nadine's porch, overwhelmed. Nadine was talking a million miles per hour, but I wasn't really paying attention. I kept staring in the direction of Jake's house. From where we sat I could see a portion of *the corner*. His house and mine were out of view.

"Hey, Aly!" Nadine said loudly, snapping me back to attention. "What else did Jake say? Anything about me?" She was coming completely unraveled.

"Sorry to say, but no, nothing. I mean, you were only there for a little bit before you took off." The excitement vanished from her face and the gleam in her eyes dulled. I felt bad, sort of. I would have felt worse if she didn't get attached to every cute guy that came along. It would only be a matter of time before someone replaced Jake. That's what I hoped, at least. Then I'd be home free.

Nadine took out her makeup bag and began inspecting her face with a MAC compact. She had beautiful green eyes. She was cute, in a childlike way, with a round face. Unlike me or our other best friend, Nicole Hamilton, Nadine had curves. She was 15, but her curves made her look 18 or older. She had the boobs we all envied.

My mind wandered back to Jake. His smell, how he looked without a shirt on, and the song he played for me the night before…

"Wait until you hear Jake play," I gushed. "You're gonna die."

"So other than all that, nothing else, not one other thing?" She sighed.

"Well, I went back over there and had, like, a heat stroke or something, and when it happened he took me and laid me down on his bed."

Her mouth hung open. I tried to be nonchalant about it, but hearing myself say it out loud, no wonder she was looking at me like I was nuts.

"Don't look at me like that, you know how long I've known him," I said, ignoring her doubtful expression. "He's like a brother. *Anyway*, let me finish without you looking at me like I have shit on my face." I sighed heavily. "So, I'm lying there and some chick shows up. I think it was his girlfriend. Her name is Rachel. He said she isn't his girlfriend, but I don't believe him. She certainly acted like she was." There, I said it. It came out smoothly enough. I only had to lie a little bit. No big deal, I told myself.

Nadine stood up and began walking.

"All right, enough. Let's go and see what'll happen today," she said, turning back to me with a devilish grin. "Maybe one of his band mates will be interested. You know they're all super cute."

I was relieved to hear those words fall from her over glossed lips. "How long have you noticed them?" I asked, sincerely curious. "I mean, dude, I've known Jake forever and I've never even paid much attention."

I really was flabbergasted at how quickly she could turn off her like switch and move on to the next guy. Our short walk to the corner had me freaking out about seeing Matt sooner than I wanted with Jake being in the vicinity.

Nadine waved her arm at me obnoxiously. "I've noticed all of them for a long time. Now come on."

We arrived at the corner, and Matt was there with Grant and Nicole. I'd had a crush on Matt Squire for a long, long time. We were all best friends, really. When I laid eyes on Matt, to my surprise I got butterflies. Wait, were the butterflies for Matt or Jake? I wondered painfully. Jake and his band mates were hanging in his garage across the street from us.

"Hey Matt," I said cheerily, waving to him. Matt skated around doing tricks with his board. His blond hair flipped and waved around with each maneuver. I tried to focus on just him and the endearing little heart-shaped scar right above his left eye. Angels must have been watching him that day, and thought him too cute to leave an ugly gash. Matt's eyes looked especially green this morning; they were shining. They used to draw me in, but not so much today. I thought back to Jake's intense blue eyes and the way he looked at me when I was lying next to him. Those were the eyes I wanted to look into.

"What's up, Alyssa?" he greeted, as I walked up to meet him. He looked over at Grant and Nicole sitting on the retaining wall, as if wondering if he was being watched. "What's been goin' on?"

"Not much, the usual. Thinkin' bout goin' to Six Flags. We talked about it, remember?"

"Yeah, that would be cool. When should we go?"

I shrugged, unsure of anything at the moment. "I don't know, whenever, you choose. We just have to find a ride."

I was having a tug of war in my head when a welcomed distraction came into view. My neighbor and classmate, Marshall Lawrence, was walking up the sidewalk toward us. Marshall was a pretty-boy, with his fashionably cut hair, unlike the other guys in my school. He would definitely be hot someday. His brothers were all good-looking too, with their almond-shaped eyes and perpetually tanned skin. Marshall was different than his brothers, though. He was slight and thin, not big and bulky.

I'd always wondered if he were gay. It seemed obvious to me ever since I'd learned what gay was. I'd never talked to him about it, but he was flamboyant in his dress and his mannerisms were feminine; it seemed it couldn't be denied. I'd always liked Marshall. He was soft-spoken, kind and funny. He took all the teasing from kids in stride, and never lashed out when being bullied by anyone.

"Hey, Marshall," I waved happily. "Wha'cha doin'?"

He waved back timidly. I could see his eyes dart from person to person around me. He finally spoke when he stopped in front of us. "Hi, Aly." He paused, looking down at his painted blue toes sitting in white flip-flops.

"Nice toe-nails, Lawrence," Grant teased.

I instantly shoved at Grant's shoulder and glanced at Marshall for his reaction. He just smirked at Grant. Grant only wore black; a uniform of black board shorts, t-shirt, shocks, and Vans tennis shoes, always, with the exception of different t-shirt graphics.

"Um, where you comin' from?" I said, trying to move past Grant's lame remark.

"Work. Um, I gotta get going though. I'll catch up with you later." He smiled softly at me and quickly moved past, waving good-bye.

My breath escaped me and I yanked my stare to Grant. "What's wrong with you?"

"What? I can't admire his paint job?" He snickered.

"Stop being an asshole." Nadine scolded, shaking her head at Grant. Their bickering continued as Nicole watched on in amusement. Matt poked at my elbow and moved away, leaning against the wall farther down from everyone else. He tossed his head at me to join him.

Then out of nowhere there was an urge, a pull. I wanted to look in Jake's direction, but I didn't. I ignored the sensation.

Scooting up next to Matt, I wondered what he wanted. "What's up?"

"Um, you wanna go to the movies tonight?" Matt asked quietly.

My heart hit my stomach. "Why are you whispering?" I whispered back.

"I don't want them to hear." He jutted his chin towards the others. "I don't need them tagging along."

The butterflies started swirling and my mouth went dry. A little breathless, I responded. "Yeah, I'd love to. I have to check with my mom though, she might have something planned I don't know about. What time were you thinking?"

"I don't know, like seven or eight. We can grab a bite, too, at the mall." He kept tossing his skateboard with his foot and glancing at me, a bit bashful. I thought it was cute. We were both nervous. This was the first time he'd asked me out without the rest of the crew. It was a big deal. I was stoked and torn.

As we all sat and leaned against the retaining wall across the street from Jake's house, out of nowhere, a white convertible BMW full of girls tore around the corner and stopped in front of Jake's house. All any of us could do was stare. I looked back at Nadine and her face fell, her hopes of flirting with the band diminished. I finally looked at Jake and he was staring right at me. He didn't look at the bright white spectacle. I thought I would faint. I looked at Nadine and she was staring at me, too. I looked at Matt, and he was also staring at me. I decided to stare at the shining arc of Envy status to take the attention off of me.

"Well, I guess we finally have something to aspire to," I muttered, irritated.

Nadine was sour too. "Yeah, if my parents had the kind of money theirs do, it would be easy." She hopped off the wall, walking over to Matt and me. Matt took off on his skateboard, doing tricks when she got too close.

"So, Jake keeps staring over here. It looks like he has eyes for you," she snarked.

I tried to laugh it off. "Ha, yeah right, shut up. I'm sure he's just wondering who Matt is. You know, the *big brother* thing."

This was all just too much for me. Now Jake wasn't *just* my next-door neighbor anymore. I sat there pretending to be into Matt's skateboard tricks, trying to come up with what to say to Nadine when she started in on me.

"So, you know…all this time Jake never paid attention to what was going on over here. Now he's watching and can't take his eyes off us, especially you," she said perceptively.

"Maybe he's watching you?" I evaded.

"Oh, yeah right, I saw him *staring* at you," she insisted under her breath. "Are you going over there? Let's go over there."

"Are you crazy? Matt's here, and those girls are there and the band…and we've never gone over there like that before." I blurted out all the reasons I could think of. "I don't wanna embarrass myself. One of those girls is probably Rachel."

"What are you talking about?" Nadine snapped. I about died. She said it so loud that Nicole and Grant looked over at us. I immediately glanced in Jake's garage, and thankfully no one looked our way.

"Shush, you spaz," I pleaded. "Calm down already. You're like freaking out for nothing. I'm talking about Jake's girlfriend. I just told you about her at your house. I just don't know which one she is yet."

Nadine slumped. "Oh, that's right." She pouted, and I didn't blame her. I felt the same way. "Yeah, I've seen them together at school. She's the one with the blond hair. I thought she was just a friend."

"You're killing me." I shook my head, agitated. "I'm not going over there."

"Calm down. What's going on with you, you're acting like…like, not you," Nadine said, glowering.

I huffed, pulling my arms to my chest. "Nothing, never mind."

Nadine just stared at me like I had two heads. It was pointless to complain. I looked back in Jake's direction. That Rachel girl was near him, and all I witnessed for the next half hour was her all up in his face. It made my insides churn.

"All right you idiots, what are we gonna do?" Grant asked. Matt skated up to me, placing his arm around my shoulder. I froze and the butterflies swarmed.

"We could go to my house," Matt offered. "My parents aren't home."

Now my stomach really flipped around. I quickly turned to face him so his arm would fall. I casually glanced in Jake's direction, but he wasn't there any longer. Only Mike and Dump remained. To my surprise, Mike acknowledged us and waved. I smiled and returned the gesture.

"Who's that?" Matt asked.

"That's Mike. Jake's guitarist, I guess. I met him yesterday," I explained.

"Ah," he said softly, looking in Grant's direction. "That's the guy that Jake picked instead of Grant."

I was reminded how defeated Grant was the night he found out Jake hadn't chosen him as his new guitarist — how I'd seen him wipe tears from his eyes, even though he tried to hide it. He'd wanted it so badly.

I sat back on the wall taking in the scene and turned to face Matt, but my eyes kept bouncing back to the garage. Mike played with his guitar, and a loud trill bounced around, echoing off the neighborhood facades like a pinball machine. He glanced over at us now and then. He was a good-looking guy, with his spikey bleached-blonde hair and tattooed arms. He always seemed to have a cigarette hanging from his lips, lit or not. I wasn't sure what color his eyes were, but he had good form. Tall, a little thinner than Jake, but, I suppose, just as good looking. There was no reason Nadine shouldn't be interested in him.

Finally, Jake and The Envies came back outside. Rachel was hanging on Jake until one of her friends, a gorgeous raven-haired chick with bright red lipstick, tried prying her away. She had a punky vibe for sure. I really liked her look. I was completely and utterly captivated by the whole spectacle. Finally they boisterously walked to their car. They looked like they were drunk or on something. Maybe they were.

"Hey, Nadine, check out that girl with the black hair," I pointed out quietly, "What do you think? I think she's cool looking."

Nadine nodded slowly, deciding. "Yeah, she's got a great look."

"And what do you think of Mike? I think he's Abercrombie status," I said, hopping off the wall nonchalantly. I planted the seed and now she was staring at him. "I think he's hot, more edgy, you know with his tats and all. I can't believe his parents allow him to get tattoos."

"I think it's hot. I can't wait to get one as soon as I move out." Nadine informed me.

That surprised me.

***

Matt was attentive, and it made me feel worse about leading him on. Watching the videos of him competing in skateboarding events blew me away. After all these years I had no idea he was so avid about it, let alone that good. No wonder he had such roughed up knees and elbows. He was sponsored by some pretty popular skate brands, and had already won several contests. He proved his insane capabilities video after video. I was impressed with how high he went in the air on ramps and half pipes, and by all the tricks he was capable of.

My phone kept making that pinging sound, telling me I had new text messages. I'd ignored it long enough. I knew it was my mom, since I was with everyone else who would be texting me. I grabbed my phone to see what she wanted. When I viewed the name on the screen, it lit up with the name *JAKE*. I almost passed out. My head immediately began to spin from the blood rushing to my brain. How could this be? I excused myself, trying not to run into the bathroom. Shutting the toilet lid, I sat there with a stupid grin on my face. I was worried it was someone playing a joke on me. I replied back:

> *- IF IT'S JAKE, TELL ME SOMETHING THAT NO ONE KNOWS, LIKE WHAT YOU DID LAST NIGHT?*

I hit send and stood up pacing the tiny bathroom. I waited what seemed like five minutes, then the ping:

> *- SLEPT NEXT TO U*

My heart raced. Oh my God. I didn't know how to reply. In those few seconds of thought, another text came:

> *- SMELLING UR STAWBERRY SCENTED HAIR*

My hands trembled. I couldn't wipe the smile from my face. Looking into the bathroom mirror the person looking back at me was flushed. I took a deep breath:

> *- HOW'D U GET MY #?*

Jake replied:

> - *WHILE U WERE ASLEEP THIS MORN I PRGRMD UR PHN. U SHLD RLY HV A CODE.*

The texting continued:

> - *WHERE R U?*

> - *MATT'S*

> - *IS MATT THE GUY W/THE SKATE?*

> - *YES*

> - *IS HE SITTING NXT 2U WHILE U TXT?*

> - *NO*

> - *MISSIN' U. WHEN R U COMIN HOME?*

I stood there with my heart in my throat and my blood pounding against the back of my eyeballs.

> - *SOON, BUT I'M SUPPOSED 2GO2 THE MOVIES W/HIM*

> - *OH, OK*

I sat on the bathroom counter waiting for a reply and I didn't get one. My heart sank. *I shouldn't have admitted anything about Matt. I bet he thinks I'm a fake.* I had to go. I had to go home. I opened the door and floated into the living room. I was numb, which added realism for my fake sickness I was going to continue to lie about.

"Guys, I'm still not feeling right, I'm gonna go home," I said weakly, for better effect.

Matt immediately got up coming over to me. "Ok, do you want me to walk you home?" he offered, concerned.

"No, I'll be ok," I assured him. "I've felt weird all day. Yesterday too. I'll be ok."

The next thing I knew, I was knocking on Jake's door like a maniac talking to myself. Jake finally opened the door, noshing on an apple. Astonishment sparked in his eyes. I guess he hadn't been expecting me.

4

ALYSSA

Jake's eyes danced and a smile peaked at the edges of his mouth as he stood holding the door open for me. I wondered what he was thinking. I was definitely, officially losing my mind. I should be admitted to a psych ward. Every inch of me wanted to hug him, but I refrained. I moved to walk past him, and he draped his arm around my shoulders, pulling me close. My reaction was instantaneous. I returned the gesture, wrapping my arms around his waist, not saying a word. Unexpectedly, his mother came in the house through the garage door, catching us mid-hug. We awkwardly released each other, putting some room between us. Her expression was warm and her eyes crinkled at the sides when she smiled.

"Alyssa, my goodness, it's good to see you," she said, throwing us a sly grin. "Come in here and talk to me. Tell me what you've been up to."

Jake and I shrugged simultaneously. As his mom turned away, I shook my head *no*, silently pleading with him.

He looked at me sideways, shoving me forward. I sighed, reluctantly walking ahead of him into the kitchen. I sat down on a stool perched next to the counter and swung my legs back and forth.

Jake cleared his throat.

"Um, Aly came over the other day with one of her friends and helped wash my truck," he explained. "Then we got to talking..."

I chimed in. "Yeah, my friend Nadine wanted to meet Jake. So I introduced them." I gulped, wondering what else to say. Then the words came flying outta my mouth before I realized it. "Mrs. Masters, I had no idea how awesome Jake's music is. I mean, I knew he liked to play, but the sound coming from your garage was always muffled, you know."

Stop blathering, I told myself. Jake had moved out of my view. Even though he wasn't touching me, I could feel his energy behind me.

"Aly, you don't have to call me Mrs. Masters. I'm no longer a Mrs. and I've known you far too long. Kate will do."

Kate Masters was a stunningly beautiful woman, with long, honey-colored hair. I marveled at her eyes. She had the same intense topaz blue eyes as Jake. Her face showed hardly any signs of her true age, no deep lines, and barely any wrinkles. I wondered how old she was. If you didn't look too hard, you'd think she was Jake's older sister.

"Are you kids hungry?" She flipped her hair off her shoulder as she turned toward the fridge.

"Yeah, actually, I am." Jake said, looking over at me and I shook my head in agreement. "Aly is, too."

"Ok, I'll make a pizza. Do you like pepperoni?" she asked me.

I nodded. "Yeah! That sounds yummy."

Jake walked over to a small TV mounted underneath one of the kitchen cabinets and turned it on. Kate stacked the counter with what appeared to be ingredients for the pizza. I was waiting for a box to come out of the freezer. She quickly explained how bad frozen food was for you.

She schooled us about sodium and the amount used to keep frozen food edible, which was way more than anyone needed for an entire day. She went on— *"if you just take some time for preparation, your health will be much better in the long run."* She preached lightly about organic food, acupuncture and natural remedies for modern day ailments. I sat there, listening, fascinated by this new information.

Jake was trying not to look bored—he'd probably heard it all a thousand times, but I asked a plethora of questions. Each time I glanced in Jake's direction, he nodded at me approvingly. I was exactly where I wanted to be.

It was cool making pizza dough. I attempted to toss mine in the air like those pro Italian pizza guys.

"Oh, you think you're fancy like that, do you?" Jake teased.

With one toss, Jake's dough launched across the counter and landed on the floor.

"I'm obviously fancier than you," I snickered.

Jake cursed under his breath, laughing and leered good-humoredly at me. I was proud of my lop-sided dough canvas. We finished our pizzas and put them in the oven. Kate disappeared into the other room.

"You can relax now, Chatter Box," he chided, moving in closer to me. "I'm not gonna lie. I'm glad you ditched skateboard boy."

I threw him a cross look for his smart remark.

"Don't forget I told Matt I might go to the movies with him tonight."

There was silence. Jake held a bag of pepperonis, tossing them one-by-one into his mouth. The anxiety grew inside me with each silent second. He walked to the fridge, grabbed a bottle of water and took a long swig. Finally, he looked at me.

"Yeah, well," he said, standing there leaning against the counter staring at me with a blank expression. I was dying inside. I didn't want to always be the one pouring my guts out. "I guess the one thing I can always count on is that you'll tell me the truth, right?"

I stood there frozen, thinking about all the lies I'd told to everyone *but* him. At the moment, his statement was true. I didn't know how to respond, so I just shrugged and he asked, "so, what's up?"

I could feel the heat rising in my face at warp speed and turned away without a word. I walked out of the kitchen to find solace alone in the bathroom. In the midst of my brain hemorrhage, I didn't hear Jake walking behind me. When I turned to close the bathroom door, his arm extended above my head, pressing into the wood, holding the door firmly in place. I'm sure he could read my face like a bright red stoplight.

Looking up at him, I wanted to kiss him. I wanted to grab his face and kiss him, like I'd seen in the movies a thousand times. His face was so close to mine, and I could smell his perfect scent. Closing my eyes, I took in a deep breath and felt both of his hands cup my cheeks. My heart stopped. He rested his forehead on mine and I felt his breath warm on my lips.

"Don't be embarrassed," he insisted, his voice was low and velvety. His hands left my face, prompting me to open my eyes. I brought my clenched fists up under my chin and considered my next words. Before I could speak, he pulled me close, hugging me, and led me toward his room. "Come on, let's talk. I'll go first, but you have to promise me you'll be honest, too. I'm probably just as nervous as you are."

I sat there on his bed, petrified. My breathing was shallow. I needed to find relief or I'd pass out.

Jake continued. "Ok. So…I've been thinking about you all day, ever since I saw you with… *Matt*. I thought about you all morning, too." He paused, getting up to pace back and forth in front of me. "I was stoked to know that we'd be hanging out, you know, getting to know each other again. I thought you felt the same way, especially after last night. Then I saw you and Matt hangin' on each other and I found myself getting… jealous, which isn't normal for me. I'm not *that* guy and it made me…uncomfortable."

I was tripping out on how open and honest he was being. Were all boys like this?

"Jake…" I reached out and touched his hand. He held it in return. He remained standing, playing with my fingers, and continued to speak.

"No, wait, let me finish," he said firmly, taking a seat beside me. "I wanted to know if you were still with him, if you were alone with him. I wanted to know what you were doing. That's why I sent the text. When you told me you were going to the movies with him…I felt stupid or whatever. Like, did I misread you? I thought we were on the same page."

I interrupted, "Jake, there's no confusion..."

He squeezed my hand. "Look, I know better than anyone that someone can be attracted to another person even when they're attached to someone else. That's why people break up most of the time; because they meet someone else they like better. Kinda like what happened with Rachel the other day. If I didn't like being with you, I would have walked you home and hung out with her."

His confession made my heart swell with excitement. I couldn't believe what I was hearing. No one in the history of my life would ever compare to him. He finally looked over at me, resuming his thoughts on the matter.

"So, you know, when you admitted you've liked Matt for a long time, it just brought to mind that maybe, while you felt attracted to me...our time these last couple of nights might just be fleeting, because of your stronger connection to Matt."

I couldn't comprehend his words quick enough to reply. His speech was a complete masterpiece.

In my stunned state I barely eeked out my next words. "You know all too well, huh?"

Jake looked at me oddly. "What? This is for you more than me, Aly. You're the one that's having this thing with Matt."

"I just feel bad, you know. Don't you, about Rachel?"

"No. I don't. Rachel has her own issues. She's a big girl. She'll get over it, eventually."

I gulped. "Ok. What else? What else makes you know all too well?"

Jake sniffed, and a reluctant grin peeked at the sides of his mouth.

"Sometimes people stay in something, even when they know it's not gonna end well, and…and some people don't ever get into anything because they're waiting on someone else, with the hopes that *that* someone will eventually come around."

"Wow. That's deep." I chuckled uncomfortably.

"Yeah, sorry, didn't mean to go all Dr. Phil or whoever." He paused, sucking in a deep breath. "So then I threw my phone down after you said you may go to the movies with him. I was bummed."

Jake looked sheepish and shrugged his shoulders.

"I guess there's your answer," I said leaning into him. I was embarrassed to look at his face any longer than a few seconds.

"I trip out on how fast this has all come on, you know, but realizing I've known you my whole life, I guess it's not so strange," he confessed.

Before I could respond, Kate shouted out that our pizzas were done. We both stood up, a bit uneasy. He put his arm around my shoulder, nuzzling me warmly as he led me out.

We ate quietly, and I chose my next words as I admired his long lashes. "The difference between you and I is," I said, decisive. "You've already been where I'm at, now. You understand what you're feeling." I knew he'd probably been there and done *that*, and every other thing in between.

Jake considered my statement and finished chewing. "Yeah, but…I can talk to you. I've never had that with anyone before. No matter how much I liked someone…" He trailed off. "I'm always boxed in. I don't know…sometimes I feel like there's this image thing I have to uphold."

Jake's voice grew quiet and he stared at the pizza crust in his hand.

"What image?"

"You know, like nothing bothers me. I don't know…it's stupid. Put it this way, sometimes I don't always do what I want to do because of what people might think. I shouldn't give a shit, but it just happens. Like this voice inside telling me—*that's not cool, everyone will think you're a pussy if you do or don't do this or that*—So I don't always do the right thing."

"I see."

I certainly did see…every perfect contour of his face that stared back at me. I repeated his words in my head and wondered what it must be like for him. I felt like I could tell him anything.

My phone pinged with a new text message.

Jake glanced in its direction. "I wonder who that'll be," he said sarcastically, bobbing his head. "I'll bet it'll be Matt."

"Shut up. It's probably my mom." I picked up my phone, and lo and behold, it *was* Matt. My stomach sank. I didn't want to admit it was him, but I couldn't lie to Jake, not ever. Not even about the smallest thing. "Ding, ding, ding, you were right. He wants to know if I'm feeling better, and if we're still going to the movies."

"What, you weren't feeling well?" Jake swooned, mocking me.

"No, I wasn't. I *was* sick. This whole thing with us has completely thrown my whole universe into a black hole. The last 24 hours? I feel totally rattled." I paused when I saw the confusion on his face. "Ok. I mean, how do I tell my friends? *Oh, I don't like Matt anymore, I'm into Jake now; and by the way Nadine, I'm sorry, I know you wanted him to like you, but he likes me now*—Really, how do I do this?"

"Wow, I didn't realize all that," he said. "So, Nadine's the reason you came over?"

"Yes, and don't look at me like that," I huffed, gathering my thoughts. My next words came out slowly. "You know, I'm totally blameless in all of this. I didn't know I would react the way I did, and feel the way I'm feeling. It's like I've been living in black and white and you're the color, the vibrant bright outline to everything grey."

I was embarrassed about my honesty, but I couldn't help myself. I stared down at my pizza crust, feeling my face get hot again.

"So, where do we go from here?" Jake said, smiling softly at me and taking another slice of pizza. "I mean I have to ask, right?"

"Like you said last night, not to read into anything? Besides, my family would die if they knew I was hanging out with you like this. You're the only one who knows."

"What were you gonna do about going to the movies with Matt if they won't let you date?"

My stomach tumbled.

"What do you think? I was gonna tell my parents we were going as a group."

"Of course you were," he said dryly, rolling his eyes, not surprised.

I sighed deeply. "What am I gonna do about Nadine?"

"Why don't you just tell Nadine how it is? She'll get over it," he said, a bit annoyed.

His solution sounded simple enough, but there was no way I was going to tell her.

"Jake, it's a girl thing—and she's my best friend, and even though she likes to flirt with everyone, she rarely *quote unquote* makes dibs—meaning she told me straight out that she likes you," I explained, pausing. "It just has to run its course, I guess."

"What are you gonna do about Matt?" Jake asked again, more firmly this time. A surge shot through me.

"I'm thinking about it, and in all honesty, I really care about Matt. We've been friends since kindergarten. He's always been there for me." Jake shook his head in understanding. "I don't wanna hurt his feelings."

"Ahhh, I guess *I'll* just have to get over it."

Jake reached over grabbing my empty plate and placed it under his. I noticed a tiny little tattoo on the side of his left ring finger, an *R*. My stomach sank. Was that for Rachel? Was he lying to me about everything?

I cleared my throat.

"You know, when I saw Rachel hanging all over you, I didn't like it either." I admitted, agitated. "What's that on your finger?"

I pointed at his finger, but only stared at his face. I watched for any indication that he was calculating a lie, something I'd learned from dealing with my sister. I recalled how easily he'd lied to Rachel about me *not* being at his house, when I was. He looked down, staring at it and then rubbed it. He shrugged and half-laughed.

"A stupid drunk night, that's what this is. It's the initial of my first real girlfriend, Renee. That night was actually the first night I ever drank, see, and look what happens."

I could only hope he was telling the truth, for truth's sake. Not that it mattered whose name it stood for. I didn't want him to lie to me to save me from bad feelings like he'd done with Rachel.

I stared at him blankly.

He tilted his head, reading me.

"Aly, I'm not lying. I'll call her and hand you the phone if you don't believe me."

Now I felt stupid.

"No. Geez. I was just wondering. I mean it *is* an R, after all." I said fiddling with the placemat. "What do you think Rachel will do when she realizes we're actually hanging out?"

"It's gonna be hard getting rid of her. Her best friend is Dump's girlfriend, Sienna Barnes, the girl with the black hair. They're inseparable, her and Rachel that is."

After more small talk about how Jake and I felt about each other, I finally sent Matt a text apologizing, telling him I still didn't feel well. I felt bad about lying, kind of.

Jake and I continued talking for hours.

5

ALYSSA

Getting my wits about me was nearly impossible.

"By the way, you have to really teach me how to play the guitar. That's the only way I'll be able to come over here so often without anyone wondering. Just my luck, my bitchy ass sister will ask me to show off my new skills," I told him.

We were sitting in Jake's living room and he picked up a guitar, handing it to me. Being too close and feeling the warmth of him, I didn't know how I would focus on learning anything. He began playing a familiar tune that I couldn't place. I marveled at how easily his fingers navigated and plucked away at the guitar strings. He strummed the melody as I searched my memory, trying to place the song.

After the first few hand contacts and body brushes, I finally calmed enough to pay attention. I didn't have to admit I was nervous—Jake could tell; he reminded me more than once to breathe. *"Aly, don't hold your breath, breathe slowly."* His voice remained smooth and even, soothing my nerves until they were completely gone.

He told me about what my first lesson would entail without ever looking down at his playing. He made it look too easy. He explained in a gentle voice that we would fo-cus on basic chords and add in very simple strumming.

"There you go, see, it's not bad." He released his hold on the guitar. "I think you're gonna be picking this up pretty quickly. You're a natural."

"Ya' think?" I chirped with excitement. "I was so nervous my fingers wouldn't get it."

A knock came at the front door, and my mood plummeted. It seemed we were always being disturbed. I hoped it was a sales person or one of those Jehovah's dudes. I heard the familiar voice and my heart stopped. I took in a deep breath and stood up, pacing a bit. Then I sat back down waving my hands in front of face as if they would help cool me off. Soon enough, the voice grew louder, and there she was. Nadine. WTF!

"Hey, it's Nadine," Jake announced. I imagined my-self bopping him upside the head. Didn't he get it? Didn't he hear what I said about Nadine liking him? We were supposed to keep our hanging out under wraps. What an idiot. What the hell was she doing here anyway? I wondered, silently fuming. My stomach acids were rag-ing. I composed myself, making like I was out of it, since I was supposed to be sick. I hoped Jake didn't forget about that too.

"Hey, what's up?" I said weakly.

"I just went to your house. Your mom said you were over here having a guitar lesson, so I thought I'd come over and check it out," she said, looking around curiously.

"Yeah, well, since I'd blocked this time with him I didn't wanna cancel, since it was only for an hour."

"Yeah, sit down, take a load off." Jake gestured to the lone chair next to him.

104

When Jake chimed in he eliminated the negativity. Nadine's eyes lit up when he spoke to her. I wanted to slap her upside the head with the guitar. I reminded myself that she didn't know how I felt about him. She should be the one slapping me around. That guilty feeling crept in again. Ugh, I hated myself. What was I going to do?

"So, Nadine, do you know how to play any instruments?" he asked.

"I use to take piano lessons ages ago," she answered, smiling. "I know how to read music, and I think it would be easy for me to learn."

"Yeah, well that'll make it much easier for you since you have an ear for the notes." Jake nodded his head. He looked over at me and winked. I was afraid to look at Nadine in case she caught that. "So, you interested in lessons?"

I almost passed out when I heard the words hurl out of his mouth. I immediately excused myself and went into the bathroom without looking at him. I didn't shut the door all the way because I wanted to eavesdrop. I could hear him back-pedaling. He was stammering. *Good*, I thought, *that'll teach him*. I laughed silently, triumphant.

Nadine was prying:

"So, how long has Aly been here? I mean, how long ago did her lesson start? Are you almost done?"

"We actually just started. My mom was here, and hadn't seen Aly in a long time."

It was killing me! He was sharing too much information! I could only imagine what she looked like, with her tits hangin', spilling out of her tank top. I had to keep reminding myself that this wasn't her fault. She was just being herself. I was the one that was the backstabber. I berated myself for the mean thoughts going through my head like a roadrunner on crack.

"Why don't you come back in an hour? We should be done," Jake suggested.

I couldn't believe my ears! What the hell was he thinking? I leaned against the door in disbelief and strained to hear more.

"I can call Mike over and I'm sure he would be glad to make a schedule for lessons; besides, he owes me. I would offer, but Aly is enough for me right now. I shouldn't even be spending the time with her."

"Oh, sure, yeah, I understand. If Mike could do that, it would be awesome."

I could hear the disappointment in Nadine's voice.

"I'm sure it'll be no prob. I just have too much to prepare for with the upcoming tour and all."

"Oh, I totally get that. Sorry, I don't mean to put any pressure on you."

She sounded sincere. Now I really felt bad.

"Hey, don't be sorry. Come back in an hour and I'll have more info. Ok? Let me go check on Aly."

Oh shit! I gently shut the bathroom door and locked it. I ran the water and wet my face. My heart raced. Even though I anticipated his knock at the door, my heart still lurched into my throat.

"Aly, you ok?" he asked gently.

"Yeah," I said opening the door, peeved. I wanted him to know I was upset. I dried my face with a hand towel, my words muffled. "Did she leave?"

He shook his head *no* and I gave him a tight, evil eye. He grabbed my arm tossing me into the hallway. He practically shoved me along the way. I put on a pathetic sick face as we rounded the corner back into the living room. I walked slowly, moving my hair from my face, which I matted wet against my forehead.

I sat on the sofa, giving a frail smile. "Hey, sorry I didn't call. I'm feeling a lot better than I did yesterday, but still not quite right." I knew she didn't care. She was probably pissed as shit at me that I crept in on her territory.

"It's ok, I hope you feel better," she said sympathetically. "Jake's gonna have Mike come over to teach me to play the guitar too."

She glittered with excitement. By all appearances, she didn't seem to be mad at me. I was cautiously relieved. I'd certainly know the truth when she had me alone.

We sat there quiet for a moment and Jake pulled a metallic blue and black pack of gum out of his pocket, offering up a piece as he popped one into his mouth. He prompted Nadine to leave by standing up and touching her shoulder. Nadine bounced out of her seat and practically danced out of the room.

"Alright, I'll see you in a little bit! Aly, I hope you're still here when I come back." She disappeared out the door. I reminded myself to tread lightly with my assumption that she'd be okay with this arrangement and considered my options while I chewed my gum.

Jake sat and put his arm around my shoulders, pulling me close. I melted into him as he leaned back, sinking into the cushions. My head bounced around on his chest when he began to chuckle.

"Why are you laughing?" I asked, miffed.

"I'm laughing at you. You have to trust that I know how to play the game, Aly."

"Oh, do you?" I said sarcastically. "Please share with me what you know about game playing, with girls."

He smiled thoughtfully and his eyes roamed my face. My insides bubbled. I tried to pull away, but he held me in place.

"Relax Aly, the Nadine thing will work out. I have a plan."

I closed my eyes relaxing, slightly. I suddenly felt his lips brush lightly against my temple and a bit of breath escaped me. As much as I wanted him to really kiss me. I was scared. My mind reeled—*what if I kissed like shit? What if I drooled all over him? What if I couldn't control myself?*

"Jake?" Our faces nearly touched. He leaned down and softly kissed the side of my mouth. My breathing instantly became shallow and erratic. The *energy* was pulsing between us. "Jake, I don't think…" As I began to speak, he gently kissed me full on the lips, and it took my breath away.

His warm, minty breath washed over my face. His lips brushed against my cheek and pressed softly onto mine again. My heart thumped a million miles per hour and I pulled back. Sensing my hesitation, he released me. My chin dropped to my chest, my eyes averted his. I was embarrassed. He lifted my chin to bring us face to face and placed his forehead against mine.

His voice was low and silky. "I'm sorry, I should have asked," he whispered, pulling me close once more. I buried my face into his neck.

"Jake, I'm the one who's sorry, I'm not…" I had trouble spitting it out. I didn't want to sound like a baby.

"Why are you sorry? Don't be sorry, that's ridiculous." He rubbed my back tenderly and moved, making room between us.

I sighed deeply, and my words came out in a burst. "Maybe I *am* too young for you. I'm not what you're used to. I know about guys like you…"

He put his finger to my mouth stopping the avalanche of dialog. "Wait, what? Guys like me?" he repeated, sounding offended. "Guys like me, what?"

"I know you're used to being with girls, and you know I wanna be there too, but…" I giggled nervously. "Wait, that came out wrong."

He laughed, throwing his head back.

"So, you wanna be what?" He teased and his eyes glimmered.

"You know what I'm trying to say, Jake, don't make this harder for me than it already is." I begged, shoving at his knee.

"Please continue. I wanna know more about guys like me." He grinned and enjoyed watching me squirm.

"You know what, never mind. I'm not gonna continue humiliating myself." I pouted.

He hugged me, sniggering. "Alright, I'm sorry. I get it, but check this out. You don't know guys like me, Aly."

Wait, what was that supposed to mean? Is he agreeing with me?

"What?"

"This thing with you isn't the same as it would be with someone I just met at a party, or someone at school, or some fan girl." He released my shoulders and placed his elbows on his knees. His head hung low and his lush hair waved over his forehead. After a long moment he continued, looking at me. "I'm in no rush with this. I don't wanna be anywhere else other than being on tour. I totally dig hangin' with you. It's comfortable."

"I still feel lame. I'm sorry I keep bringing it up."

"Don't be. I'm perfectly fine kissing you like we're still in 6th grade." His smirk grew more pronounced.

I could have been insulted or embarrassed, but I wasn't. I was relieved. The thought of French kissing him made me nervous beyond belief. Even though I'd dreamt about doing it more times than I could count. Actually doing it with *him* was another story.